Sinful Woman

James M. Cain

G·K·Hall&C̣o.

Boston, Massachusetts
1993

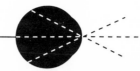

**This Large Print Book carries the
Seal of Approval of N.A.V.H.**

Copyright © 1947 by James M. Cain. Copyright renewed
1975.

Published in Large Print by arrangement with
Harold Ober Associates.

G.K. Hall Large Print Book Series.

Printed on acid free paper in the United States of
America.

Set in 16 pt. Plantin.

Library of Congress Cataloging-in-Publication Data

Cain, James M. (James Mallahan), 1892–1977.
    Sinful woman / James M. Cain.
        p.   cm.—(G.K. Hall large print book series)
(Nightingale Series)
    ISBN 0-8161-5462-7
    1. Large type books. I. Title.
    [PS3505.A3113S5   1993]   92-27528
813′.52—dc20

Chapter One

The revolving door revolved, and into the bright mountain morning stepped a girl in slacks, a red ribbon around her hair. She was an uncommonly pretty girl, with blond curls showing that glint of gold which cannot be obtained with chemicals, and a skin with high, dappled flush. Yet her good looks went beyond prettiness, and often touched beauty. For the actual moulding of her face was plain, with a wistful, haunting sadness that reflected the soul of every homely girl in the world; but she had a curious trick of seeing far horizons, of smiling at invisible stars that gave her a rapt, exalted expression. In contrast with this, her figure was wholly sinful. It may have been part of the reason, indeed, for the spirituality of her face, for its breathtaking voluptuousness could not be concealed under any sort of clothing, and condemned her, no matter where she went or how, to the role of nude descending per-

1

petual public staircases; thus she moved as though withdrawn into herself, with an abstracted, Godivanian saunter that was aware of nothing nearer than the sky.

She set off at this gait now, but at once noticed the little knot of children across the street, who had stopped playing and begun staring at her the moment she left the hotel. Smiling at them, she crossed over, shook hands, asked names, and distributed chewing gum from her handbag. Then she recrossed the street and resumed her way.

She had gone only a few steps, however, when she heard her name called, and turned to behold a spectacle as unusual in its way as she was in hers. Estimating conservatively, one would have said there was 6′ 2½″ of man approaching, mounted on 2½″ of bootheel, and mounting 1′ of hat, making a rough, overall height of 7½′ of lumbering, graceful lankiness. But this 7½′ had strange, not to say bizarre aspects. There were the flapping, workworn, cowhide chaparajos, covering long, indeterminate legs; a holster over the right hip, from which protruded the butt of a big pistol; a heavy flannel shirt, featuring 3″ X 2″ blue-and-red checks; and the fawn-colored hat already noted, which was big as well as tall, and probably

2

held 12 gal. Even as this was being swept off in a fine, Rocky Mountain arc, she was staring in unconcealed wonder, and said: "Darling, I see it, but I still don't believe it. Nothing personal, but I just don't think they make them like that anymore."

"You mean these chaps?"

"I mean all of it."

"I been breaking a colt, and they save pants. Well, I started out as a packer, and kind of got used to the clothes that kind of work calls for."

"What's a packer?"

"Oh"—with a wave at the snow-capped Sierras in the distance—"he packs stuff up in those mountains. Miners, prospectors, or just plain dudes, they've all got to be packed, or they'll be getting a little hungry along about the second day out."

"And that was your start in life?"

"I owned eight mules before I could vote."

"And now?—No, don't tell me, I see it all, as it were a crystal ball. Now you rope. You rope, with gags. Last year you M.C'd. all the rodeos in the Western Panhandle of Texas, and one in northern Wyoming. And when I get back to California, you want me to get you a part in a Western. Well, here's where it gets good: I'm going to do it. So far as

3

I'm concerned, you've got what it takes. But hold!—a horrible thought enters my mind. You don't sing, do you? You wouldn't yodel Home on the Range? You're not that kind of a cowboy?"

Had she been less concerned with the clothes, she might have noticed his eyes, which were the most arresting, as well as the most Western thing about him. They were a light, china blue, with a look of bland, childish innocence in them, until something troubled him, when they seemed to develop the eerie faculty of seeing right through whatever they focused on. They focused now on his hat, which he was pulling through his fingers in such a way as to cause the silk binding to make a harsh, rasping noise. Then, rather slowly, he spoke: "Miss Shoreham, I'm not no kind of a cowboy. I'm Sheriff of this county, and as I saw by the papers it was your last day in town, I was going to ask you to step over to my office and sign a couple of legal papers. But as it was to be more of a joke than anything else, it won't be necessary, and I'm sorry if I bothered you."

The 7½′ grew to 8′ as he bowed, put on the hat, and strode off in the direction of a group of public buildings down the street.

She went as far as the clear mountain stream that boiled its way through the city, then stopped and stood frowning down at the water. Then she turned, walked back to the hotel, and went in. To the clerk she said: "Can you direct me to the Sheriff's office?"

Three startled deputies, reading the morning paper, jumped to their feet when she came in, and she spent a minute with them. Like most actresses, she took delight in the commotion she caused, and had a real affection for rough men. Unlike most of them, she had a marvelous memory for names, for she had been a restaurant hostess, and had a mind like a card index. As with the children, she asked names now, smiling a little at the surprise she would cause when, on leaving, she would get all the names straight. Then she asked the Chief Deputy, whose name was Flynn, to announce her to his chief.

The Sheriff seemed a little confused as she strode into his private office, and he covered something with a filing basket before taking her proffered hand. The chaps, gun, and hat hung on a tree now, and he had put on a coat. But it was not the change in his appearance which caused her to stop in the middle of her greeting and stare down at the

5

desk. It was something familiar about one corner of the picture under the basket. She pulled it out: it was a large photograph of herself as Edith Cavell, her most celebrated picture role. Lifting the basket, she found other photographs under the big one: snapshots, blownup candid camera studies, one or two items she had never even seen. She said: "Are these the legal papers?"

"They might be."

Picking up a pen, she leaned over on her elbows. "What's your name?"

"Parker Lucas."

She signed the big picture, "To Parker Lucas, the high-mindedest Sheriff I know, with best regards, Sylvia Shoreham." Then on the others she wrote. "To P. L. from S. S." It took a minute or two, and when she was done he said, "That was most kind."

But his eyes were still cold and she looked away. After a short silence she said, and I want to apologize.

"There's nothing you got to apologize for."

"I trifled with the law."

"The law wasn't after you."

"I trifled with a man."

"Men generally get trifled with."

"Nevertheless, I have to apologize. For

shooting past a big moment in my life. For not knowing it was a big moment. I think, from these pictures, from something I felt after you left me just now, that I mean a lot to you, more than you'd be willing to admit, except that I'll make you admit it before I get done. And I treated you like—somebody to chatter at for a minute, and then get rid of with some kind of brusheroo that wasn't too much trouble. Most of the time, if you're in pictures, you can't help that. It's just part of the business. But sometimes it's just dumb. That's why I want to apologize."

If his heart had softened, his face gave no sign. He had got up the moment she came in, and she now went over to him, her mouth thick, her eyes glinting in anger. "Listen, you big lug, Sylvia Shoreham doesn't apologize to every county Sheriff, you know."

His face lit with a delighted grin. "Don't she?"

"Hello."

"Gee you look sweet."

She gave his necktie a yank that left both ends dangling down his shirt, then deftly retied it so that instead of looking like a double-wrapped breeching, it looked like a necktie. As she did this she gave a startling take-off of his recent remarks: "Ah'm she'ff

7

dishere county. Ah'm root'n-toot'n-shoot'n man. Ah'm old-time pack'n man, bit haids off eight hot rattlers 'fore Ah could vote. Ah'm bad hombre. Cattle rustlers, train robbers, bandicks, varmints, and bums, take notice and *lam out!*"

"It's murder, but keep on. I just love it."

"When did you start collecting Shorehams?"

"Three-four-five years ago, when you first came out. You made quite an impression on me in those days."

"Oh in *those* days."

"Even if I don't like your last pictures."

"Not even Meridian 1212?"

"Specially not Meridian 1212. That cheap, gum-chewing, lolly-gagging telephone operator you were in that picture just made me sick. You know the best picture you ever made?"

"Cavell?"

"The Glory of Edith Cavell was the best picture that ever *was* made, if you ask me. I saw it at least twenty times, and I know it by heart, some of it. And how anybody that could make a picture like that could turn around and make some of this junk you've been in, like Sarong Girl and Love Pirate, and I Took the Low Road and Swing

Chum. I don't know, and specially I don't know how you could do it. You called it right just now. You mean plenty to me, or did anyway. And I don't mind telling you, here lately you've been giving me the colic bad."

He wasn't smiling, but had turned solemn, and so in a moment did she. After a long, grave silence she said: "You believe in pictures, don't you?"

"I believe in the good they can do."

"I'd like you to know I hated those parts just as much as you did. But, I've been working for men that don't believe in anything about pictures but the money they can make out of them, and Sylvia Shoreham in a tight sarong sells tickets. I had to wear that sarong. It was that kind of contract. But now, I'm happy to say, that's all over." Haltingly, she explained a little about her commitments, and the relation they bore to the man who would be her husband for an hour or so longer, or until the court of this state handed down its decree of divorce. "So you see, it's a little more complicated than you think. It's been all mixed up with a marriage, and a contract, and a lot of personal things that got pretty messy, but that you had to do *something* about. That's why today is a pretty important day with me. Everything's been pretty well straightened out, and while the papers will say divorce, it'll really be a little Declaration of Independence, so far as I'm concerned. Sort of a Battle Cry of Freedom. This afternoon Sylvia Shoreham starts a new life."

"I'm glad to hear that."

"So you can keep right on talking."

"I probably said too much already."

"You said what I've been needing terribly to hear. I think you believe in a lot of things that Hollywood never heard of, and that I've got to learn all over again if I'm going to do with my life what I want to do with it. So you can begin exactly where you left off. Tell me more about Cavell. And I promise to listen to every word you say."

Before he could say, however, his phone rang, and the conversation indicated an impending visitor. She wigwagged that she was going, but he shook his head. When he hung up he said: "That wasn't anybody but the major. I'm going in the army as soon as I can make my deal, and we generally argue an hour every morning. They'll make me a colonel if I go with the mules, but I'm not keen on remount."

"What do you want?"

"What I want is to fly. I love it. But I'm

10

thirty-two and that's too old, and besides a man ought to do in this war what he can do. Moving stuff in rough country is what I'm good at, so I guess it's the S.O.S."

"Will you have lunch with me?"

"Will a colt eat sugar?"

"I have a sister with me, that's seen me through this ordeal of the divorce. I'd think I want her to meet you. She's younger than I am, and prettier."

"She must be a sight."

"Then, I'll expect you? At the hotel? Around one?"

"At one sharp I'll be there."

They gave each other a long smiling glance, and then she flitted out with the light skip of an actress who has taken a great many exits. She was a patter of feet, a wave of the hand, and a ripple of hair as she went through the outer office; just the same, three names hung in the air as she was gone, and three delighted men looked at each other and said, gee that sure was one swell gal.

Chapter Two

She was really going to a lawyer's, to await whatever formalities might be indicated on

11

his return from court. But on her way she stopped, to indulge a weakness that had developed during her stay in this city where she was obtaining her divorce: the hazarding of $100 at games of chance before taking up the serious business of the day. The establishment that she entered never closed, its employees working in three shifts of eight hours each, and while it was typical of such places locally, it differed from the great gambling houses of the world, having little of the cold elegance that usually goes with them. Rather it offered gambling along cut-rate lines, and indeed, with the sunlight streaming in, it had some of the petty glitter that one associates with a downtown drugstore. Painted in all sorts of colors, and with all sorts of mirrors in their navels, were whole batteries of slot machines, operating at 5-&-10¢ limits, and having their licenses framed beneath them; along the walls were electric Keno boards, and in front of them long troughs filled with corn, for keeping score. Wheels of fortune were everywhere, some of them the noisy old-fashioned kind, with a leather finger clicking between the whirling pegs and real money under their numbers; others silent, a revolving light serving all necessary purposes. Every hour on the hour a functionary circulated with a bucket, into which the clientele dropped the tickets that had been issued them for drinks bought at the bar; a few minutes later there was a drawing, and the holder of the winning number received $5.

Then of course, there were the roulette wheels, faro layouts, poker tables, dicing pits, and other mahogany-and-baize installations for the carriage trade, as well as racing results for all.

Sylvia Shoreham's arrival was an event, even in this pre-occupied place, and the proprietor hurried forward to meet her. His name was Tony, and he was a grandson of one of the Italian charcoal burners of the sixties, who settled the Sierras to furnish various cities with their fuel, and then left the horde of descendants who so largely populate that part of the country today. Like most gamblers, he took pride in not looking like a gambler; he wore the habiliments of a prosperous undertaker, and would have been astonished to learn that God doesn't see much difference. His rocky face breaking into a smile, his thick body inclined at a deferential angle, he advanced briskly, counting chips with his own lily-white hands. "Baronessa!"

"Just an hour or two longer, Tony."

"Ah, today is the day?"

"It's being done now, let us hope. The Baroness Adlerkreutz becomes plain Sylvia Shoreham again, and only all too glad to be back with the vulgar herd."

But before she could accept her chips, an attendant hurried up, a girl with a green baize apron over her stomach, and said: "There was a message for you, Miss Shoreham. The hotel called, and said your husband is in town, and wants you to ring him at this number."

She handed Sylvia a slip and went back to her dice game. Tony said: "Come into my office, Miss Shoreham. You don't look so good. You look like you better sit down quick."

He led her into a redwood-and-leather office, seated her, and opened a window. But when he produced a bottle of brandy she waved it away. "No thanks, Tony. I'm not sick or anything. It's just—"

"Bad news, hey?"

"I had no idea he was here."

"He trying to block your divorce?"

"I don't think so. I don't see how he can."

"Maybe wants money."

"I imagine it's nothing but some foolish

last-minute stunt to get me to change my mind, and incidentally sign a new contract with that picture company I've been trying to break away from for the past two years. Something silly, but nothing serious. But, I don't want him around! I don't want him around the hotel. I don't want him around my sister. I—"

Tony's eye caught the slip of paper in her hand, and he gave a little *clk* of surprise. "You know that number, Miss Shoreham?"

"No, I don't."

"That's the Galloping Domino."

"Oh, on the road west."

"*My* other place."

"*Your*—What's he doing out there?"

"Looks funny."

They peered at the slip, and he said: "I tell you what we'll do. I've got to go out there anyway, so you come with me, talk to him, see what he wants. Then if it's bad you stall him and I'll slip back to town. Hazel and I will move you out of the hotel to my house, and you'll be there where nobody can reach you with a subpoena, a camera, or anything at all."

"Oh, dear, I've asked somebody to lunch."

"O. K., my wife'll serve the lunch. And

15

you'll love my little daughter Maxine. She's just about Hazel's age, acts in all our productions here in town, crazy to get in pictures—"

But at this Sylvia's smile became a little glassy: picture people are usually wary of girls crazy to get in pictures. Quickly she said, "I'd just love it, Tony. I've seen Maxine and I think she's the sweetest thing in this town. But—first of all, let's find out what he's up to."

They drove out the main highway to a place that looked like a cross between a country club and a Kentucky thoroughbred farm. It was a rambling white building surrounded by trees, with a low, shingled roof, green shutters, and brass doorknobs. Inside, it was a replica of the place they had left, except that it was smaller, and a little gaudier, and a little more cut-rate.

As they turned in at the gate, Sylvia pointed to a green car out front, and he drove around back. They entered through a side door that led to Tony's office, which was exactly like the one in town except that it had green leather chairs instead of red. In the door at the other end of the room was a little metal slot, the kind that speakeasies used to have. Tony opened it, peeped out.

Sylvia peeped, and her face hardened as she spotted a lone player at one of the blackjack tables, who handled his cards with nonchalance and chatted flirtatiously with the pretty dealer. Tony looked incredulously at Sylvia. "Not *that* guy?"

"Of course. Why?"

"He's been in every night for a week."

"Here? At the Galloping Domino?"

"He's a regular."

The bartender went by with bottles. Opening the door, Tony called him, and he came in. "Jake, that guy over there, the one playing blackjack with Ethel—you know anything about him?"

Jake looked and said, "Sure, he comes in."

"What names does he go by?"

"Search me. He's some kind of a foreigner. He said call him Vic, so that's how we left it."

"What's he do?"

"Fishes most of the time, I think. Took a shack by the river, couple miles up the line. He's got plenty of dough."

"Send him in, Tony."

Jake and Tony went into the casino and Sylvia sat on the edge of the big desk, her face set, her eyes narrow. In a moment a burst of waltz music entered the room, transformed itself into a man, took her hand as though it were a water lily, brushed a kiss up on it, wafted it gently to her knee again, and stood murmuring her name, as though such a vision of loveliness were more than human fortitude could endure. He was a rather large man, but made with such grace that he almost seemed small. About his lean hardness there was something of the cavalry officer; about his small hands and feet something of the ballet master; and about his bright black eyes something of the pimp. But his mouth was poetic, and it throbbed now, like the throat of a robin, as he kept repeating "Sylvia-Sylvia-Sylvia" in a soft, sibilant whisper.

She looked at him for a time, then lit a cigarette and crossed to one of the leather chairs, sinking back in it and hooking a reflective knee over one arm. Then she said: "Believe it or not, Vicki, I'm a little glad to see you. And my hand has a little tingle spot on it, where it was kissed. Even when I know the whole routine frontwards and backwards, it still does things to me.

"But it is no ruttine! Is from 'ere. Is from 'eart."

"What do you want?"

"To see you, Sylvia! No odder t'ing. To

sing one song, to break one glass, to blow one kees, before comes a end!"

"The worst of it is, it could be true."

"Of course is true! I say myself, Vicki, what you do? You sit 'ere! You let time go by. You act like damn full! Tomorrow you lose Sylvia, you no do one t'ing! I jump in car, Sylvia! I drive in one night! I swear you, I live 'Ollywood last night, no stop even buy gas! I see thees place, I coon wet! I coon wet, had to see you Sylvia. I jump out! I stop car 'ere thees place, I jump out, I phone huttel, I—"

"You lying Lithuanian heel, what do you want?"

"O. K., Sylvia, I tell you."

"And not so loud. And not so funny."

"Is all true! I must see you! . . . but why I call up? Was afred! Was afred you live thees place before I find you! I say to myself, I most 'ave thees t'ing—"

"Have *what?*"

"Thees ring!"

She looked down at the ring that was still on her finger, a plain gold band with steel oval on which was cut a coronet. Without a word she slipped it off and handed it to him. When he had kissed her hand passionately again, she said: "I would have sent it

19

to you. I don't know why I haven't already, except it's one of those things you just don't have a box to fit. But why the phone call, and the fuss, and—"

"I get marrit again, Sylvia."

"You—*what?*"

"Yes. I get marrit today."

She got up, lifted the phone, asked that Tony be paged for her. When he came in she said: "Tony, a bottle of champagne."

"Yes, Miss Shoreham."

"No, Sylvia, I coon permit—"

"Tony, champagne. And be sure it's very expensive champagne. Champagne in every way fit for a bridegroom-elect—"

"Miss Shoreham, don't tell me—"

"Not I, Tony. My husband."

"Ah yes, champagne."

With a deferential bow to Vicki, Tony left the room. Sylvia said; "Does she live here, Vicki? Is that why you took the shack?"

For a long, worried moment he stared at her. She laughed. "You didn't expect to get away with that midnight drive from Hollywood, did you?"

"Who tell you about shock?"

"You really want to know?"

"Yes, plizze."

"The bartender."

20

"Jeck?"

"Yes."

"When?"

"Just now."

"Nobbudy else?"

She laughed again. "No, Vicki, nobody else. So if delicious naughtiness has been enjoyed by all, I don't know a thing and you're perfectly safe."

Tony came in presently, with an ice bucket, a bottle with gold foil on it, and two glasses. When the bottle had been well-twirled in the ice, he cut the wire, winked as the cork popped, and poured. At the toast to happy days he backed out, and Sylvia said: "Do you know what I thought, Vicki?"

"Ah, Sylvia! I frigh'n you, yes?"

"I thought it was Phoenix Pictures."

"You mean I—pull treek?"

"Yes you, lovely you."

"Sylvia! Coon do soch t'ing you."

"But, I was ready for you. And that reminds me, Vicki, I'm afraid I have just the teentsy-weentsiest bit of bad news for you."

"Bad news for me?"

"I'm afraid you won't be a producer for Phoenix much longer, marrying actresses Dimmy Spiro wants for the sarong trade. Since Phoenix wouldn't do the right thing

21

by me I did the right thing by it, and picked up a few shares that Dimmy forgot about, enough to give me control. So next week you and Dimmy and me are all out, and Phoenix gets sold to Metro or Warners or whichever company it is that wants to buy it. And all three of us are free, or will be. Isn't that nice?"

Vicki looked as though he had been hit with some singularly horrible nagaika. He winced, closed his eyes, breathed deeply. Then: "Sylvia! Why you do thees to me?

"I do notting to you! Only lahve you!"

"I think you've forgotten that little contract we signed together, with the extra page in that I swear I never saw until later, the one that gave me to Dimmy for seven years, with no way I could get out of it if he kept on paying me the miserable little salary it allowed me. And that gave you a great big salary as producer of my pictures, although the only thing you had ever produced up to then was girls for Dimmy's parties. Do you remember about that? Do you remember how I begged you for a release from that dreadful contract?"

"Sylvia, why we no make new dill?"

"It's impossible, Vicki."

"We 'ave soch fine, big plan for you—"

"I wouldn't sign with you and Dimmy if you were the last producers on earth. And just so neither one of you try any tricks with the S-S Corporation, that nice little dummy company you got me to organize, I might as well tell you I haven't got that stock I bought, not one share of it. It was bought for Hazel, and it's all in her name, and there's no way Phoenix can be saved, or you and Dimmy can be saved, or I can be made to work for you!"

"Sylvia! You brek me 'eart."

"However, enough of that. Who's the bride?"

"Is girl I met. Nize girl."

"She lives here."

"Lil while only."

"Ah, the divorce question again?"

"Si and so and sa."

"Do I know her?"

"Shoon be surprise."

". . . I do?"

"Is Hezzel. Is your seester Hezzel."

Chapter Three

She had been holding her glass up to the light, watching the bubbles drift up the stem, but now set it down. Then she stared at Vicki as if she were trying to realize what he had said, to sort it into its various implications, to grasp what it meant. He, his face momentarily in repose, his eye everywhere but on her, seemed to have changed a little; the glow had left him, and he suggested still another characteristic of the Middle Europe that had produced him: a capacity for slippery schemes, not prosecuted in offices, where Americans cut throats, but in the boudoirs of women and other haunts of the helpless. His dark good looks were quite sinister under her stare, and he merely shrugged when she burst out: "Vicki, you can't seriously mean what you say?"

"Min? Sure, I min. Hezzel nice girl."

"You must be—gagging or something. You can't go through with it and face what hell will have waiting for you."

"Hell? Can be. Who knows?"

He was distressed but vague, and she stood up, the tears glittering in her eyes. "I don't speak of myself. I suppose it was too much to hope for, that I could get rid of you and Dimmy and Phoenix all in one day. But why did you have to pick on Hazel? You know she's practically an institutional case right now? You know—"

"Then why you no take her to court?"

"In other words, if she's not herself, then I ought to have put her away. And if she is herself, she's perfectly free to marry you, and the stock is yours, and I'm yours, to make sarong pictures as long as Dimmy, tells me to—and then *you'll* have her put away."

"But, I *lahve* her, Sylvia! I—"

One pretty fist caught him in the mouth, and its fluttering throb gave way to a tight pursing, as he touched it with his handkerchief to see if it was cut. She began to stride up and down with a slow, feline glide. As she talked, her breath came in deep inhalations and her fingers laced and unlaced: she wasn't a woman giving way to emotion, but like one trying to repress it, and the agony of this effort gave a measure of what she felt. "You—bird of prey. You're no more capable of loving her than of loving me or any woman in your life. To you, none of us mean anything except what you can get out of us, and once you had your big reunion with Dimmy and he showed you how to cash in on the hand-kissing and the dancing and the title, that was our bad day. And especially a bad day for any girl named Shoreham. I think I'm going back to my trade, Vicki.

25

Waiting on the table is a lot more respectable than working for you and Dimmy."

"Yes is ver' nize work."

"So that's where she's going."

"You gambol so moch, Sylvia."

"Yes, I've gambled a lot. After I got her out of California, away from the chartreuse and the B-and-B and cointreau you kept filling her up with, she had a crackup and I had quite a time with her. And then when she wanted to drive up in the mountains, because they made her feel good and helped her get back to normal, I was only too glad to let her do it. I couldn't go with her. They made me feel giddy and light-headed and sick. So, I let her go alone, and to have *something* to do while I was hanging around here, I gambled. I gambled $100 a day, quite a lot, but nothing to what you and Dimmy cheated me out of these two years. And all that time she wasn't driving in the mountains at all. She was meeting you—"

"Sylvia! I see her two-three-four time."

"You've been coming to this place a week, and what places did you go to before that? I know, now, that it was liquor I smelled on her breath, and not cactus candy as she said. Thanks for that, Vicki. You know it's the worst thing in the world for her, but you

26

didn't stop at it, did you? Not if that was the way to keep her coming to that lovely shack of yours."

She continued her restless pacing, seemed to get older as her face took on a desperate, haggard look. He remained motionless, perched on the edge of the big desk, staring unwinkingly at nothing. With wolfhounds at his feet, peasant girls behind him, a banker at one side, trying to collect his money, a dead deer on the other, head hanging limply down, a falcon on his finger and a feather in his cap, he would have made an excellent oil painting of *Europe and How She Got That Way*. He barely moved when she stopped suddenly and said: "This isn't your think-up, Vicki. It's too good and you haven't got the brains. I see Dimmy's fine Hungarian hand in it. Is he here?"

"Dimmy? Can be. I—"

But as though in answer to her question, the door opened and three men entered. One was short, fat, and pale, and looked oddly like an obese penguin. One was small, thin, and freckled, with unnaturally blond hair and light shifty eyes with no lashes on them. He looked like an albino rat. And one was tall, lithe, and sun-burned, with delicately-carved features and luminous eyes, so luminous they suggested the moon-agates that marble players use as shooters. He looked like a horse who aspired to lofty things, such as popcorn instead of oats. All three advanced on Sylvia at a noisy run, their arms outstretched, their mouths forming big grins. She backed off with a snarl. With no apparent sense of embarrassment, the tall man and the freckled reduced speed to a walk, then strolled over to a framed photograph of the Johnson-Jeffries fight, and stood studying it. The third man, the short fat one who looked like a penguin, came to a full stop, and stood looking at Sylvia as though she had cut his heart out and he wished she would give it back. Then he said: "Sylwia! Is me! Is Dimmy!"

"You think I'm blind?"

"But, Sylwia! This is no way to act! Here we come! Make a big surprise for you! Bring fine script! Queen of the Big House—ah Sylwia, you'll love this little B-Girl that goes to prison to save the fellow she loves."

"I can see her now."

"And we have another surprise! Tell, Vicki!"

Vicki, however, kept silent, and in a moment Sylvia sat down, covered her face with her hands. After a while she went outside, stumbled aimlessly around, spied Tony's car, got in it. There, in a moment, tiptoeing up to the window, Tony joined her. "Bad, hey?"

"Worse than I could have dreamed."

"Who are these others?"

"The one in the beret is Dimmy Spiro, head of Phoenix Pictures. The tall one is La Bouche, his production manager. The little one has a last name, I guess, but I don't know what it is. He's called Benny the Nib. He's a check forger that Dimmy brought in as a writer, to do a story for me called Queen of the Big House. And they're up here to—"

She broke off, thought a minute, as though to decide how much she wanted to tell this man anyway, then told him what was brewing in short, jerky sentences. When she mentioned Hazel he whistled, evidently having long since guessed the girl's mental condition. Then he said: "Then it all checks up."

"What checks up?"

"Jake heard a little more. They got in last night, and stayed with your husband in his shack. The idea was, they were to lay low until your divorce was granted, then the girl your husband is to marry—Hazel—would come out and they'd be married. But your

29

husband he wanted some sort of ring he'd given you, so Hazel could be married with it. He wanted to catch you before you left town, but he hadn't had a phone put in the shack, so he came here. They're pretty sore. They didn't want you to know until it was all over, and they thought the ring could wait."

"Not a Baltic baron's ring. It's his soul."

"They're a funny bunch."

"You're telling me?"

Mr. La Bouche appeared at the back door and asked Tony if he had a shine boy. Tony called, and a Mexican youth came out of the garage at rear. Mr. La Bouche told him to go inside, and step on it. Benny came out and announced that if he had no saddle soap, he needn't come in at all. Mr. Spiro came out, flicking a handkerchief against his soft leather boots, and inspected the can the boy had by now taken out of his box. It was at this point that Vicki came out, leaned close, and whispered something to Mr. Spiro. When Mr. Spiro nodded, Vicki started around the club, first stopping to lift Sylvia's hand out of the car, press a kiss on it, and put it tenderly back. When he had gone, Sylvia said: "Tony, will you lend me the car?"

"You mean now?"

"I'm going to follow him in. I'm going to follow him straight to wherever he's meeting her. I'm going to stop this horrible thing if it's the last thing I do on earth."

"Well—I guess so."

"Give me the key, quick."

Following the Baron, however, wasn't quite as simple as it looked. She was only a few yards behind him as he turned out the gate, and for a few hundred yards up the road she held him in view. But then, as she matched his rapidly mounting speed, the needle leaped to 60, to 70, to 80. At 82 she missed a truck, lost her nerve, and pulled back to a sane rate. The green car disappeared around a curve, then vanished altogether. She drove a few moments uncertainly, then leaned forward with evident purpose. Back in town, she drove to a small office building. When she hurried into a lawyer's office on the second floor, and asked for Mr. Daly, the girl at the switchboard seemed mildly annoyed. "Well, he's been expecting you all morning, Miss Shoreham. He's had to break two engagements outside, and I've been trying to reach you."

Mr. Daly, a tall, thin man with sandy hair,

was amiable enough about her tardiness, but when she blurted out that she wanted the divorce stopped he frowned, announced frostily that this was a most unseemly time. Briefly, leaving out psychopathic details, she explained what was afoot. He interrupted disagreeably: "I can't impress on you too strongly the thought that it will be practically impossible to straighten out your affairs, particularly your professional contracts, until you get this divorce. Under the community property laws of California, your husband can—"

"I want this marriage blocked!"

"Why *shouldn't* he marry your sister?"

She didn't answer.

He got up, took his hat, started for the door. His phone rang and he came back. When he hung up he put his hat back on the tree. "Your decree was entered an hour ago."

"Mr. Daly, what can I do?"

"Nothing."

"Can't we phone the marriage license bureau and—"

"They have no authority to refuse your sister a license, if, as I understand it, she's of age. Besides, she can be married anywhere. Why don't you talk to *her?*"

Dismally, Sylvia drove back to the hotel, but there the clerk shook his head. "Your sister went out, I'd say it was over an hour ago, Miss Shoreham. No, she didn't leave any message, or—" He broke off his phone, then held his hand. "It's for you, Miss Shoreham. Would you like to take it here?"

Trembling, she took the phone, but it wasn't Hazel, it was Tony. "How's it going, Miss Shoreham?"

"Just terribly."

"I just called up to leave word that you needn't bother about sending the car out or anything. If you'll just leave the keys at the desk I'll have somebody drop by for it."

"Thanks, Tony."

"Oh, and one other thing. That ring."

"Ring? What ring?"

"It's the ring I've seen you wear, the one with a coronet on it. I thought perhaps it's the same one your husband—"

"Yes, it is. What about it?"

"He must have forgotten it, or dropped it, or something. One of the girls picked it up in the office. I'll bring it in—"

"No, no! Listen to me, Tony!"

"Yes, what is it?"

"He won't get married without it. He'll be out after it, and I might still be able to stop them. Say nothing to anybody about it, and don't give it up, even to him. I'll be right out, as fast as your car can take me."

In the casino of the Galloping Domino a fat little man sat playing roulette with one hand, holding a coffee cup with the other, and extending both feet to a Mexican boy who was just finishing an extensive job of polishing two soft calf boots. Behind him, a tall man and a little man stood admiringly, exclaiming over the acumen of his bets, which had now netted him an agreeable profit. In the office, a girl sat at the redwood desk, fingering a ring that lay on the blotter before her. On the steel oval she noticed tarnish, rubbed it on the virgin blotter. It made marks. Possibly to find a smaller blotter she opened the center drawer, then the righthand drawer. But this she closed quickly, for she had glimpsed something never far out of sight in gambling houses: the cold, oily sheen of pistol barrels and rifle butts.

Outside, a car with its lights burning turned in at the gate, a girl at the wheel, a man beside her. He jumped out, ran into the casino. She continued around to the side, turned the car so it faced the road, stopped, and waited.

"All right, Vicki, here's your ring, and I guess you win. What's the deal? A new contract? Sell Dimmy the stock? Do Queen of the Big House? Whatever it is, it's all right, if you'll only promise not to go through with this ghastly thing."

"Is O. K., Sylvia. We mek new contract, big money for you, vary big money. Sell Dimmy a stock, yes, he pay fine price. Pay one twanny five. Is nize, ha? Do Quin a Big 'Ouse. Ah, Sylvia, is fine picture!"

"Just one little thing."

She went over, stood very close, looking him in the eye, and spit in his face. He took out a handkerchief, wiped his cheek, and stood looking at the floor a long time. Several times he started to speak, and couldn't: of all the insults she had offered him in the last hour, this alone seemed to have reached the quick of his nature. His mouth had just started to throb when there was a light tap, and the door to the casino opened.

Chapter Four

The girl who now entered the room in a stagey green dress was a by-product of

Hollywood that gets little attention in print, but that occurs with unhappy frequency in that enormous catch-basin of talent: the feeble residuary legatee of such life as remains in a family after some prodigious child has been born. Rarely on public view, they are to be seen in homes, clubs, and dressing rooms, these pale, futile, carbon-copies of greatness, having no identity of their own, no existence except what they can suck from somebody else. Most of them, however, are happier than the rest of us manage to be, for it is the irony of life that those whom they worship commonly love them to distraction, would do anything for them, try to do everything for them. The real story of many a celebrated actor, if anybody were cruel enough to print it, would turn out to be, not the romance that his fans talk about, or the success he has made in his profession, but his unremitting effort to bring Christmas into the life of some dimwit brother who means more to him than anything else on earth.

How much this girl actually looked like Sylvia it would be impossible to say. Her figure, while not quite the sculptor's dream that Sylvia's was, was quite striking nevertheless, and similarly formed. Her hair, whatever it's original color, had been bleached to the same shade of blondness as Sylvia's, though it lacked Sylvia's little glint of gold. Her eyes, a medium blue, weren't so far from the gray of Sylvia's. Her features, certainly, bore rather a marked resemblance. Yet, one suspected that actual similarity went no further than it commonly goes between two sisters. What made her look like Sylvia in so startling, in so shocking a way, was the slavish imitation of Sylvia that she indulged in, with every slightest grimace. From her walk, to her facial mannerisms, to the little wistful smile, to the sad look into distant spaces, she was Sylvia, at least in her own imagination, and could never, for one waking moment, be anybody else.

She gave a little exclamation of delight at seeing her sister. "Has Vicki told you, Sylvia?"

". . . Yes, Hazel, he has."

"Are you going to forgive me?"

"You haven't done anything to me, darling."

"I wanted to tell you, but I was afraid."

"Vicki has something to tell you."

"No plizze, Sylvia, you tell."

Sylvia's arm went around her, and into her

eyes came a queer look, like the look that comes into the eyes of a cat that smells chloroform. In a frightened, throaty whisper she asked what they meant, but it was a long time before Sylvia could answer. Then, miserably, she said; "Vicki's not going to marry you, darling."

". . . Why?"

"I asked him not to."

"But *why?*"

"I didn't think it would be good for you."

"You mean my trouble?"

"It wouldn't work out."

"But my trouble is all we ever talk about. He's going to take me to Vienna when the war's over, and there are doctors there that know all about it, and it's going to be a simple matter for me to get cured."

"It might not turn out that way."

"But, Vicki—"

"Isn't really much of a psychiatrist."

Vicki, his mouth throbbing now in a veritable flutter, came over now, murmuring Hazel's name in a frenzy of compassion. He patted her on the head, said: "I never know thees t'ing till Sylvia today she tell me. Todayheute I on'stan all. Is moch better, Hezzel, we do like Sylvia say. All lahve Sylvia, no? All t'ink Sylvia know best?"

For answer Hazel opened her handbag, took out a cigarette. Then she began walking around. In spite of Sylvia's reminders that the doctors had told her not to smoke, she kept snapping the cigarette against her thumbnail, in nervous, ominous taps. Then she moistened her lips, in the way Sylvia moistened them before beginning a big scene. Then she spoke in the quiet, vibrant way that Sylvia spoke when these scenes opened, the way that suggested patience, restraint, all the idealistic things she stood for. She said: "What I want to know is, why did you agree to this? What did she say to you, Vicki, that made you decide to give me up?"

"I merely told him—"

"No, please. Let Vicki talk."

"Say you nuts. Is all."

"It couldn't have been that. You knew that already."

"Din on'stan about thees t'ing."

"And it couldn't have been about the money."

Sylvia looked up, startled, and Vicki seemed to have turned to wood. Hazel went on: "Certainly it was nothing of a business nature. We've talked this over many times, and both agreed that Sylvia would be much better off to stay with Phoenix, and I had

agreed to turn the stock over to you as soon
as we were married, since I better than anybody else know what's good for her. What
is this business?"

"Can be."

"Vicki, I don't believe you."

She was sad, patient, detached, every inch
Cavell rebuking a young nurse who had
failed to bring a soldier his canteen of fresh
water. After a pause in which she looked out
the window with a little compassionate
smile, she went on: "There's only one other
thing she could have told you . . . Dirt! Dirt!
. . . Rotten, filthy dirt!"

This was the celebrated Shoreham change
of pace, the pregnant whisper with which
Sylvia could get more terrible punch into a
scene than most actresses could get with a
hundred foot of screaming. Sylvia, who had
sat down, started to speak, didn't. She
leaned back, closed her eyes. She acted as
though she had been through this many
times before, and knew there was nothing
to do but let Hazel have her head until she
ran down, when perhaps she would become
manageable. Hazel went on: "Oh yes, there
have been men in my life. I'm human. All
too human. I didn't think it hurt anybody.
That I could have a little romance, a little

touch of beauty to look forward to. Little did I dream that my own sister—"

She broke off and stood with face twitching, tears welling into her eyes. This was another Shoreham specialty: a dead-end stop with tears, not with the assistance of a cut and glycerine, but straight into the camera, with real tears glittering in her eyes. After a long look at distant inspirations, Hazel went on: "My own sister. She's been kind, you say. Yes, kind she has been. She feeds me, gives me a bed to sleep in, buys me shining raiment. She buys me silk, and costly furs, and fine motor cars, and little trinkets, to prove she loves me. But I, I have known the joy of giving, too. I have given a life. Little do they realize that I too might like to be an actress. Little do they know that I too crave admiration, that I too might like my name in shining lights from Maine to California, from China to Timbuctoo, from pole to pole and sea to sea and tiny isle to greatest continent. And it might be mine. Who knows? Am I not young? Am I not fair? But no. I renounced my share of the sun that *she* might shine. I gave up what might be mine, that she might have what should be hers. I, God help me, I loved her, and my reward was—this—"

A wrenching monologue that was usually given Sylvia in Reel 5, this was spoken without so much as one motion, standing behind a desk. The usual way to close it out was not to attempt to finish it, or make a great deal of sense out of it, but to give Sylvia's matchless voice its chance as long as the scene would hold, as well as her incredible capacity to speak with no pantomime whatever, then let her do some trivial thing to bring the story back to everyday realities. Hazel again tapped her cigarette, opened the middle drawer, as though looking for a match. She tried to close it, but she was rapidly losing muscular coordination as her break progressed, and it stuck. She pushed against it with her hip, and her dress caught in it. Yielding for a moment to blazing rage, she banged it with her fist, got it closed. Then she opened the righthand drawer.

Sylvia was still sitting with her eyes closed, a look of terrible pain on her face. It was Vicki, who had wandered restlessly around the room, and was now behind Sylvia, who saw what Hazel lifted out of the drawer. With an exclamation he leaped forward, for the gun was leveled straight at Sylvia. Sylvia opened her eyes, didn't

42

move a muscle. She said: "I'll be looking at you, Hazel. Every night."

"No!"

"*Yes!*"

The crack of the Shoreham voice was followed by a terrible stare. Hazel looked away, as a cat does from a human being, whimpered, lowered the gun. Vicki, who was standing within an inch of her, took it, put it back in the drawer.

Sylvia said: "Damn you, Vicki." Then she got up, went over to the wall behind her, and said: "You'd better go now. Because I don't know how long God will give me strength to stay away from that desk. From what's in that desk. Go. Don't be here when I turn around."

Chapter Five

Compared with Sylvia's glowing twenty-five, Spiro's age was sallowly middle; compared with her slender curvation, his contours were distressingly blimpish. Yet he was still under forty, and in spite of pallor, fat, and baldness, he gave off something describable as magnetism. Spiro wasn't his name, but it was a fair approximation of his mother's name, she having been Hungarian; his father's Lithuanian name was wholly unsayable and unwritable, at least to Americans, and he had dropped it. He had started life as stable boy on the estates of the late Baron Vladimir Alexis Gustavus Adlerkreutz, near Memel, where his father had charge of the cattle and his mother had charge of the cheese, curds, and butter. Respect for the *Herrschaft* was a prominent feature of the Spiro household, and young Dmitri early learned the deep bow that a peasant must give them, and the correct way to take off his hat to them, and the rigid stance that was required in speaking to them, to be relaxed only in case of critical moisture in the nose, when relief with the back of the hand was permissible. He had one friend, however: the young Vicki Adlerkreutz, son of the baron, and owner of a fine Shetland pony.

After the last war, however, his education was interrupted, for he returned to Buda-Pest, whence he had been taken as a child, and got work tending horses in one of the circuses there. It wasn't long, however, before he persuaded the management to let him do a comic turn with the clowns.

Comedians are the business men of the theatre; indeed comedy is a business, requiring bookkeepers to keep track of its jokes, its emoluments, and its taxes. After that, his rise in show business was rapid, as was his increase in weight, and acquaintanceship with actresses of the grand, or Viennese style. Soon he had a company, first in Buda-Pest, then in Vienna, a theatre, and a monocle. But then came certain upheavals, and long before Anschluss he left hurriedly, for Paris. There he tried to get started again, but succeeded only in losing such money as he had been able to salvage. He came to Hollywood, and had been there only a few days when he met, at Vine and Selma, his former friend, the young Victor Alexis Olaf Herman Adlerkreutz, now baron in sight of God and all men except Hitler, who had taken his estates. It was the greatest moment of his life when Vicki recognized him, kissed him on both cheeks, dragged him into the Brown Derby, and borrowed $5. For the rest of his day he relaxed, and permitted his head to swim, and inhaled the iridescent beauty of the sunshine at the reflection that he, Dmitri Spiro, a peasant boy, had been thus treated by Adlerkreutz, a baron of Lithuania, with full seignorial rights over the peasant girls of his domain, and no doubt a great many actresses too.

From then on he and Vicki saw each other a great deal, and within a week had taken an apartment together in Beverly Hills. Then the ex-comic, the business man of the theatre, saw the use to which he could put his handsome friend. A young girl was just coming up in pictures, could be made into a star. She had been, not a waitress as she usually said, but a hostess in a Wilshire Boulevard restaurant that bought time on the air for a little lunch-hour feature called Your Favorite Celebrity. When the regular announcer failed to show up one day, she had taken over the mike, and managed it with such tact, wit, and charm, that overnight she was a celebrity herself. Then she got a part in a picture. So one night at the Mocambo, Dmitri appeared at her table with a sketch he had made of her, and asked her to sign it. It was small, risque, and good. Laughing, she signed and the next night he presented his friend, Baron Adlerkreutz. The month after that she made a picture, The Glory of Edith Cavell. The month after that, not quite sure how it happened, she was the Baroness Adlerkreutz, rather pleased at the title, wholly captivated by Vicki, and a little surprised, but not unduly alarmed, to find that somewhere along the way she had signed a lot of contracts.

From then on, Dmitri was successful indeed. Like most of his colleagues from the Danube country, he had a gift for the cute; i.e., for sentimental little situations with a slightly salacious twist, lending themselves to uniforms, peasant bodices, twirling slippers, and czarda music. Sometimes he used the same plot with goona music and South Sea atmosphere, with sarongs instead of bodices; once he switched to swing, with B-girls' dirndles instead of sarongs, and the story became Love Pirate. Anyway he cut it up, it was the same old hotza; it didn't make actresses but it made him; Sylvia slipped, but he grew rich. Now, as he sat here in this Western gambling hall, his appearance implied his career. The soft calfskin boots, now glowing under the Mexican boy's fingers, suggested his present eminence, as well as his start among the horses. The whipcord riding breeches, fitted to his rotund rear, suggested the movies that now engaged him. The full duellist's shirt, puffed at the throat by a silk handkerchief around his neck, suggested the mokos of Paris. His monocle, as well as his brown silk beret, suggested all the cafes of the world.

He was playing the first four and the first twelve, risking two 25¢ chips at each spin, and greatly enjoyed Mr. La Bouche's admiration, and Benny's admiration, to say nothing of the admiration of the little blond croupier who was serving the table. He frowned when he saw Vicki come in, but was reassured when the sunny smile broke in his direction, and Vicki rattled something at him in German about 'wir beide,' which seemed to mean that Hazel was with him, and that the scheduled ceremony was not far off. Tony bustled up, told Vicki his ring was in the office, if that was what he came for. Dmitri went back to his game with zest, and paid no more attention to what went on in the forward part of the establishment, even when Mr. La Bouche held up his finger as though he heard something, and the croupier spoke of the backfiring of trucks, and how the road ought to be renamed Artillery Avenue. Presently, Benny said: "There goes Vicki."

"Is she with him?"

"Must be. Tail light's burning."

"She's nuts."

"No law against driving with the lights on

if she likes driving with the lights on, is there?"

"No law gegen to be nuts."

Sylvia came into the casino and Dmitri looked at her in surprise, for he hadn't known she was here. She said: "Dimmy, if you want to see that personal appearance contract you'll find it back of Tony's desk. I just signed it in red ink."

Then she hurried outside, and he watched her uneasily as she stepped into the sunshine. Then, becoming aware of what she had said, he knit his brows in puzzlement, turned to Mr. La Bouche and Benny. But they, with that sixth sense that is a special characteristic of Hollywood, had quietly vanished. The boots were almost done now. Paying the Mexican he got up, walked around the end of the bar, approached the office. Throwing open the door for the majestic entrance that befitted his station in life, he strode into the room. He was well inside before he noticed there was nobody there, and stopped. Then he looked at the desk, which had nothing on it but a blotter, a paper cutter, and an ashtray. He looked out the window, to where Sylvia stood at the river's edge, and took a step or two in that direction, as though he were going to call

49

to her, find out what she had been talking about. Then he gave a low, quavering moan. Then he turned green, and sat down in one of the big leather chairs.

Dreadful, hammering seconds went by before the door opened and Tony came in, faultless in his double-breasted black suit. Dmitri got up, forced a smile, lunged at what was intended for casualness. "Beg pardon, plizze. I'm looking for the proprietor."

"I own this place."

"You, Tony?"

"Tony Rico is my name.

"Spiro mine. President Phoenix Pictures, big Hollywood company. Could I speak to you one minute?"

"What about?"

"I'm in a little trouble."

"What kind of trouble?"

"Telling the truth I don't know. I was not personally here. But nothing serious I give my word honor, epsolutely. Friend of mine, Baron Victor Adlerkreutz, fine fallow, fine family, one finest families in Europe—is hurt.

"In what way?"

"I think—shot."

"And what do you want of me?"

"Listen, Tony; listen, old fallow, listen to

me, plizze. I want you to let me get the Baron out from here. I want we get him to a private hospital, get a doctor quick, fix it up what we say, so when the police come, and all those damn reporter, we don't have any mess."

"Afraid I couldn't do that."

"Tony, you don't want no mess either!"

"Your friend's dead."

Tony motioned toward the desk and added: "Or so I think." He glanced at the small mirror he had in his hand, polished it with his handkerchief, went behind the desk and knelt down.

In a moment he stood up and came over to Dmitri, holding up the mirror. "You see anything on that?"

"No."

"Neither do I."

He went to the phone, picked up the receiver, jiggled the bar. Dmitri seemed to come out of the trance that had half enveloped him and jumped for the instrument. Tony stepped aside and motioned him back to his seat. But, Dmitri kept grabbing, until the phone was knocked off the desk and Tony had to let go or have the cord torn out by the roots. He swore hotly at Dmitri, who paid no attention.

51

"Tony! Not yet! Don't call the police till I talk to you!"

"Sorry, this is nothing I can talk about."

"Yes, Tony."

"Listen! I don't know where the hell you come from, but in this state we got laws."

"Tony! Don't you get it? I'm a producer! If this mess comes out, it ruins me, ruins my life, ruins my company, ruins my star!"

"Once more: There's nothing I can do for you!"

"Then do it for Sylvia!"

"You trying to tell me *she* shot him?"

"Who do you think?"

Tony stared incredulously at Dmitri, who seized the chance to pick up the phone, set it on the desk, and clap the receiver in place. At once it rang. He answered. "Hello. No, nobody called. Fell off the desk. Sorry, plizze."

He set the receiver in place, held it with both hands. Sylvia came in, her bravado gone. She sat down. Tony, after looking at her, was no longer incredulous. He went over to her. "We've been having an argument, Miss Shoreham. About something that's happened. I've got no choice. I've got to report it."

"Yes, I know."

"It's none of my affair. But after what's been going on, it don't surprise me any. I want you to hear me say that, Miss Shore-ham."

"Thanks, Tony."

"A jury may feel the same way."

"I'm not that far yet."

To Dmitri, a little wearily, Tony said: "You needn't hold on to that phone. There's twenty-two extensions in the place, and I can call from any of them."

Dmitri leaped for him, clamped arms around his neck as a drowning man might. "Tony, you don't know what I say even. It's not the jury. It's *Hays!* So, jury say O. K., is swell, hey? Is like hell. Hay say, *mess* is *mess* and rub her out. Tony, I got one million pingo-pangoes tied up in this face! One million I swear, for Sugar Hill Sugar, first picture I make all my own money ! If this mess comes out I can't release! It breaks me, breaks my company, breaks Sylvia—"

"It's tough, but I can't—"

"You want money? I'm rich, I—"

"So am I!"

"I buy your place, Tony! How much—"

"It's not for sale!"

"Tony, give me ten minutes! Give me five minutes! I've got my production manager here! He can make it accident! He can make it—"

"Mr. Spiro, maybe you've been in the pictur business so long you don't know how the rest of the world is. I'm a gambler. To you, maybe that's a low tout, somebody to be bought. In this state a gambler is as good as anybody else. He pays most of the taxes, he runs a straight game, he's a leading citizen. And if you think you can—"

"O. K., ruin me. I don't care."

Tony started for the casino, first unwinding Dmitri from his neck and flinging him to the floor. But for a moment, in this straight-shouldered march to rectitude, he hesitated, broke step. It didn't seem possible that Dmitri, prone by the desk, could see. Possibly he heard. At any rate, he rolled over, jumped up. "What is it, Tony? Only say!"

"My little daughter."

"Yes, your little daughter!"

Tony stood like a man of granite. Then, with even more emotion than Dmitri had shown, he went on: "My little girl Maxine, that's got more talent than any actress that ever lived; that's sent her picture to every scout for every agent in Hollywood, and that not never even got an answer to your letter;

54

my little girl that's crazy to get in pictures—could you make her a star?"

"Tony! Ask something hard, something that will show how I feel for you! If she's not cross-eyed, I make her Garbo! If she *is* cross-eyed—"

"She's not cross-eyed."

Having leveled one mountain, Dmitri turned to the Everest that sat motionless in the chair.

But to his astonishment Sylvia looked up wearily and said; "Yes, Dimmy, it was an accident."

Chapter Six

The clock in the hotel lobby crept to 1:05, to 1:10, to 1:20. The tall man in the cowpuncher's hat, who marched up and down, was a stranger to the clientele, the smart women who would get their divorces in a quiet, discreet way, then take their departures noisily, with orchids; and they regarded him somewhat humorously as they made their way to the dining room. There was nothing humorous, however, about the way the clerk regarded him. Sheriffs, in his scheme of things, were problems to be got rid of at once, if not sooner, and at the first inquiry for Miss Shoreham, he had begun paging that lady all over town. After each call he would give a report, with conjectural matter on where it would be advisable to try next. It was during one of these speeches that Inspector Cy Britten, of the city police, strolled up, set his elbows on the desk, and stood listening. Then he smiled in a sad sort of way, and said: "Parker, have you got a date with that picture actress?"

"That would be my business, I figure."

"Are you by any chance taking her to lunch?"

"Are you by any chance bothered about it?"

"No, Parker, not that I know of, though I freely admit that when she sashays up the street every morning I generally peep out the window of my office and keep on peeping. It's only that your office said you were here, and so it's my duty to inform you that there's been a shooting out at the Galloping Domino, and that it's out past the city limits in the county, and that as a matter of fact a couple of your men have already left for there, and that it's plainly your duty to go."

"And that makes you happy?"

"Well, somebody's got to take this girl to lunch—"

"And it might as well be you, hey?"

"As a matter of the courtesy of the police department, I just thought I'd wait here, and inform her of the unfortunate circumstances that have led to the disappearance of her luncheon pardner, and then, as the least that any gentleman could do, to—"

"You just thought it all wrong."

"I'm willing to bet—"

"This is how it's going to be: I left my car down to my office, not expecting to need it, and now, unfortunately and alas, I got no way to get out to the Domino without I commandeer the first car I can get. So as I see your car sitting out front, I hereby deputize you to do the job. *This* man can inform the young lady."

Driving out, the Sheriff learned more of the details. The call had come first to one of the hospitals, which had sent an ambulance, with interns and orderlies. When the doctor had found the victim was dead, he had called the city police, mistakenly supposing the Domino to be within their authority; they had rung the Sheriff's office, relaying the facts and offering whatever help might be needed. The Chief Deputy, after asking the loan of police photographers, had dispatched his own motorcycle officers, called the Coroner and police magistrate who also served as marrying justice, and also as an undertaker. In addition to their photographers, the city police had sent a brace of uniformed patrolmen, in a patrol car, to put themselves at the disposal of the Sheriff. So that when he and Mr. Britten turned in at the Domino, there was quite an array of official cars and motorcycles, to say nothing of an ambulance and an undertaker's truck.

At the door, a state policeman met them, and after saluting the Sheriff said: "We closed him down, pending and until. Such a mob jammed in here as soon as the radio give it out, on account of this picture actress, that—"

"On account of *who?*"

"Sylvia Shoreham. It's her husband that got it, and from the way they've been piling in here you'd think—" He broke off, marched out to the gate, and held up his hand to a car full of boys that was turning in. "Just keep right on. Keep right on and don't stop. This is not no cow-roping contest. I said beat it."

The boys drove off, and the officer led the way inside. To the Sheriff, Mr. Britten said:

58

"Lucky, wasn't it, that I didn't stick around to take the young lady to lunch?"

"Was, kind of."

"Things generally turn out right."

Inside, a white, tight-lipped Tony awaited them, and took them into the office where the police, Mr. Flynn and one other deputy, the Coroner, an undertaker, a doctor in white uniform, and two orderlies crowded back against the wall while two photographers took pictures. The late Baron Adlerkreutz was not lying as he had been a short time before, when he was an unseen presence behind the desk while Dmitri and Tony had their desperate argument. Now he lay in the middle of the floor, beside a few crimson drops on the linoleum carpet, the gun at his side, a tan silk handkerchief knotted in the trigger, and a white silk handkerchief knotted in the tan silk handkerchief, and fastened around his leg. Near him, and seeming to enclose him, were two ashtrays, two chairs, and the water cooler, on top of which was an electric fan. The Sheriff walked over, bent down, and peered. To Mr. Flynn, the Chief Deputy, who walked over close, he mumbled: "What's the idea of the handkerchiefs?"

"That's what we're going to find out.

They'd been having some kind of an argument about a picture scene."

"Who was having the argument?"

"The picture men. He was a producer."

"They here?"

"In the bar."

"Bring them in.

"If you'll take a tip from me, you'll walk to them where they are. Two of them are all right, but one of them, the one that seems to be boss, he didn't do so good in presence of the body. He kind of cracked up. He—"

"O. K."

Motioning Tony, Mr. Britten, the Coroner, the undertaker, the doctor, police and deputies to follow him, the Sheriff led the way into the bar, now deserted except for Mr. La Bouche, Benny, and Dmitri, who sat huddled at a table, and an officer who sat reading a paper. Mr. La Bouche jumped up and began arranging chairs, to be assisted at once by Benny; But Dmitri sat where he was, huddled in the posture of a man having a chill, and watching in some sort of oblique way, as though his nose were a side-vision mirror in which he could see what was going on. Tony made brief introductions, sat down, looked at his finger nails a moment, then said: "All right. Get going."

Dmitri drew a long, trembling breath. He said: "Sharf, Excellenz, I hope you don't take it personal I feel so upset."

"Not at all, pardner. Now shoot."

"Yes, quite so. We came here last night, me, my production manager, Mr. La Bouche, and my special writer, Mr. Benny Zitt."

"These guys?"

"Yes."

"Go on."

"We came to talk about a moving picture. You heard of me, yes? I'm Dmitri Spiro, president Phoenix Pictures, strictly class product, make only the best. We came to see our star, Miss Sylvia Shoreham, and talk about a picture. She was to get a divorce today, it meant a new start. Vicki was her husband, but all are good friends, fine friends—friendly friends."

"Get to the shooting."

"We talked about the picture, and there was one scene Miss Shoreham, she didn't like. She is a girl in prison, and had to shoot another girl, and didn't like. She said, Dimmy, is impossible. She said, Dimmy, my public will not let me do this thing. Then she walked by the river to cool off."

"Was it hot?"

61

"She was sore."

"What then?"

"So then Benny, he had an idea. He said, Mr. Spiro, she shoots the other girl, but it's accident! She finds the gun, she hides the gun, she puts the gun under the bed, but has no bad conscience gegen other girl. But the other girl sees the gun, gets the wrong idea. So they *straggle!* They straggle like in Destry Rides Again, only better. Then the gun goes off. It's accident, but who'll believe it? But, Vicki, the Baron Adlerkreutz, he said, 'Yes, Dimmy, but out in the audience, how do we know it's accident?' Then Mr. La Bouche here, he said: 'I show you, Vicki. It is so simple, you laugh. But wait a minute, I have to have a gun, or you won't believe it.' So we go to Tony, ask plizze may we borrow a gun?"

The Sheriff looked at Tony, who licked his lips and said: "I keep seven guns out here, on account of our heavy stock of cash, four rifles and three pistols, all registered to me and all under permits I got on file. I didn't want to lend them any gun. I don't want to lend anybody a gun ever. But they were friends of Miss Shoreham's, and she'd been such a good customer and all, and they acted like it was important, so I took out the clip

62

and handed over the automatic I keep in the desk.."

"If you took out the clip—"

"I must have forgot the shell in the barrel."

"Pretty careless you're getting."

"Sheriff, if Mr. Spiro feels upset, I feel it double, because I ought never to have lent the gun in the first place. I thought I threw the ejector and snapped the trigger, that's all I can say; but a wholesaler's man was waiting for me out back and—"

The Sheriff nodded at Dmitri, who went on: And so, Bushy, he showed Vicki how we can do the scene, so Sylvia will love it. He say 'Vicki, girls fight till dresses are torn to rags, and maybe Sylwia don't look good in a scene where her dress is all torn off. So one piece of the dress, one piece of the other girl's dress, catches in the gun—the trigger. We cut in, show the dress caught in the trigger, but the girls don't see it. So, Sylvia almost has the gun. She twists the gun from the other girl's hand, but oh—oh!—oh! People see the piece of the torn dress pull tighter, tighter, tighter—and *boom!* The gun goes off, and there is the other girl dead on the floor. So we tie one henadkerchief to Vicki's leg, one to the gun tryger, tie the henadkerchiefs together. Vicki takes the

63

gun, I grab it, twist his hand. Bushy, he stands by the camera, which was an electric fan on the water cooler. Bushy, he say, 'come around slow now, so it's in close to the camera.' So we come around slow, handkerchiefs tighten, Vicki say, 'Ah yes, I see now, is very good, yes, yes—come up very slow'— and *boom!* There was Vicki on the floor, and I can't believe it. I say 'Vicki, Vicki, speak to me.' I say—"

"O. K."

The Sheriff, who had evidently found this recital a little difficult to keep up with, knit his brows and in a moment said to Mr. La Bouche: "I didn't see any signs of a fight."

"What fight?"

"Well—?"

"Oh, they didn't do the fight, if that's what you mean. We allowed for that. A fight, it's like jungle stuff, it's a cutter's job anyway. You shoot five hundred feet, or whatever you need, and he puts it together. All that mattered was the torn dress and the gun. So we laid it out how that would break. We figured the cell would be nine feet long, five feet wide, with two out for the bunk. So we marked the set with the ashtrays and chairs, set up the camera over the water cooler, and started her going. I mean, it was an electric fan. The henadkerchiefs were the torn dress."

The Sheriff asked a number of questions of the doctor, checked the routine work that had been done by his men and Mr. Britten's, asked the Coroner if there were questions he wanted to ask. The Coroner wanted more information from the young interne, and was pretty exact about rigor mortis, the extent of internal bleeding, and such things. He said he would be ready for the inquest tonight, if the autopsy showed nothing to extend the inquiry. The Sheriff nodded to the undertaker. "O. K., you can move him. Hold him for autopsy and the police will instruct you. You can open any time, Tony."

Departure of the body cleared out quite a lot of vehicles out front, to say nothing of many uniforms inside. It gave Tony a chance to set his office to rights, and the undertaker's truck was hardly out the gate before he had charwomen at work in there, and was busy himself, setting things in order. When the room was restored to its former condition the Sheriff asked: "Is Miss Shoreham here?"

"I had the maid take her to the ladies' room."

65

"Will you ask her to step in?"

"Right away, Sheriff."

Her astonishment, when she saw him, was complete. He went over, took her hand, and led her to a chair. "You have a time remembering I'm Sheriff of this county, don't you?"

"All I saw was police."

"They help. But it's my case."

"I'm sorry about the lunch."

"I too. I was there waiting."

"I kept thinking about it, believe it or not."

She had let her hand stay in his, and now leaned her head against his arm with the trust of a weary child. "I guess I wanted to be with somebody that loves me."

"You think I love you?"

"Yes, I do."

"Well, you're right."

He sat on the arm of her chair, and put his arm around her, and she caught it in her hand and held it close, and cradled her head against his coat. They sat that way a long time. Then he said: "What happened?"

"I don't know what happened. I was over by the stream, and I haven't got it straight what they tried to tell me. They were rehearsing some kind of scene."

66

"They said you didn't like it."

"It wasn't that. It was them."

"I kind of wondered about that part."

"It didn't make any difference how they did it, I wasn't going to do the picture or have any more to do with them. They could just have well—never started their rehearsing.

She began to cry, and he knelt beside her and wiped her eyes with his big bandanna, and blew her nose.

Then he got up, went to the window, stood for a long time looking over toward the mountain stream. When he spoke it was with the utmost casualness:

"Who killed this man?"

She stopped crying suddenly, and he turned around and looked at her. Then she said: "I did."

"Why?"

She started to talk, and rehearsed the events of the morning. At the end she said: "I'm not ashamed of what I did, though I'm not proud of it. I love my sister more than I love anybody. She's not responsible, and what he was about to do, what he would have done, was a shocking, horrible thing. I feel I did right. It was the only way out that I could see."

"What did your sister say about it?"

"I don't know if she knows it yet. I suppose she must, but I haven't heard from her. While we were talking, Vicki thought I might go out there, where she was parked just outside the door here, and get her to come with me, and take her away from him. Or, I guess that's what was in his mind. Anyway he went to the door and told her to drive in and he'd meet her at the hotel, and she went."

"Why did Spiro make it accident?"

"Hays office."

"That's right. I forgot."

"If I get smeared, Spiro can't release Sugar Hill Sugar. It cost him a million, and if it stays in the can he's ruined."

"Now, I get it."

Presently he asked, "And why did *you* make it accident? They couldn't lie to me, if you didn't back them up."

"My sister."

"I don't understand you."

"My sister loved this man, and I love her. There is nothing I won't do to prevent her from ever finding out what I did. Don't try to use what I've told you against me. I want you to know the truth, but if you try to convict me, I shall say I never told you any such thing, and they'll believe me. I'm not

68

one of the leading actresses of the world for nothing."

"Will they believe *her?*"

"She knows nothing to tell."

"Do you remember the ending of that picture, The Glory of Edith Cavell? Where Cavell marched to the wall for something that was done by somebody else?"

"Vaguely. Why?"

"I remember it very well. When she was before that court, telling her story, she looked a lot like you looked just now. You remember the court didn't believe her?"

"I never saw the court scene."

"You—*what?*"

"Except for the shots I was in, the whole courtroom sequence was done in retakes and I never saw them."

"The court didn't believe her, but shot her just the same to bust up her organization. She didn't know it, but the man she was trying to save, the one that was more important than she was, was already dead. So the court shot her, knowing she hadn't done what they were trying her for. The chief judge of the court hated it, and that was the most awful scene I ever saw in a movie, where you and him were facing each other there. He looked like he loved you as much as I do. It's funny you don't remember that."

"It begins to come back to me."

"I thought it would."

He considered, said: "I'm taking you back to your hotel, and for the time being I'm not putting you under arrest, and I'm not putting you under guard. I could, but I'm holding everything in this case till I talk to your sister."

"Now, I'll tell you something. I love you, and I think you're the only man I've ever loved. Don't forget that, judge."

"I won't. I'll take you back to town."

They rode with him in Mr. Britten's car. At the hotel, Mr. Britten suggested they enter through the kitchen and go up in the service elevator, as such a crowd of reporters, photographers, fans, and cops were visible inside, evidently waiting for her, that they might have trouble getting through. But when the Sheriff went up with her to her suite they found it empty. Sylvia, leaving him in the sitting room, went into her bedroom to phone the desk, and when she came back she looked frightened. "She's not here."

"Where is she?"

"She didn't come back here."

"Did you send her back to California?"

"No, I didn't."

"Then don't worry, we'll find her."

He went down in the service elevator again, climbed into the car. But when Mr. Britten learned of the dragnet that must now be put out to find the missing girl, he gave an exclamation. "I knew there was something funny about this. And that girl, I heard about her when I began talking to the gamblers, but they didn't have a word to say about her."

"She's daft."

"She's—What?"

"Not all there in the head. I doubt if they even saw her. From what Shoreham said to me, she just follows along, and waits in the car, and does what she's told, and nobody pays any attention to her. Just the same, she's driving around somewhere. I want her brought in, and Shoreham does."

"Did it strike you they were covering up?"

"In what way?"

"It all checks up, I guess, or will when we get our lab reports in. And it was just about the kind of cock-eyed thing that does happen. But, I had the feeling that every time I turned my back they were looking at each other."

"Did you figure on suicide?"

"Yes, I did. There were powder burns, and that puts it within the ten-inch rule. And, I always said, if cops have made it a rule they won't consider suicide from firearms unless there are powder burns, they ought always to consider suicide as a possibility when there are powder burns. And she got that divorce, and she's a good-looking girl, and maybe he was stuck on her, and maybe he was tired of living. But why would they go to all that trouble to cover up?"

"Account of her, maybe."

"They're taking one awful chance."

"She's worth big dough to them. And maybe she's a little daft too. Maybe she's the kind that would go and join the Lithuanian Red Cross or something, so he didn't die in vain."

"You breaking it open?"

"I don't know. We got to find that girl."

Chapter Seven

Mr. George M. Layton, of the Southwest General Insurance Corporation of North America, sat in his midtown office planning his afternoon, his manner suggesting the jut-jawed determination that a field marshal might show, counting his reserve of tanks. He proposed to call on six newly-arrived divorce seekers, named in the newspaper clippings that lay on his desk, and sell them, or try to sell them, Southwest General policies. This was something he did every day, but it wasn't something to be approached perfunctorily, as just one more job of salesmanship. It involved, as he often told the luncheon club, of which he was a member, the most careful sort of planning, the most rigid attention to the probable peculiarities of the prospect, and even due regard for special conditions, such as weather. So he sat at his desk, a compact, red-haired, freckle-faced bundle of aggressiveness, dictating memoranda to Miss Jennifer, his secretary: the notes that would not only assist him in his sales talk, but form the basis of the "presentation" that Miss Jennifer would prepare, bind in imitation leather, and stamp with the prospect's name, as the give-away for the second visit. He frowned slightly when the phone rang, but suspended dictation as she stepped into her anteroom to answer. "Home office calling, Mr. Layton."

"*Home* office?"

"Well it's Los Angeles. It must be—"

"Put them on."

When the call went through he barked: "Contact! Southwest General of N. A.! Layton talking!"—this being his idea of a telephone gambit, as indicating on-the-jobness, make-it-short-ism, and close-the-dealation. The voice at the other end, taking cue at once barked back: "Contact! Greetings George M. Layton! R. P. Gans talking!"

"*Who* did you say?"

"Gans! Vice President for Claims!"

"Oh, yes of course, Mr. Gans."

Mr. Layton's voice, which had been so dark, firm, and confident a moment before quavered a bit at such overwhelming eminence. Mr. Gans went on: "You got that Shoreham flash?"

"You mean about the divorce?"

"I mean about the murder!"

"The—*what?*"

"Baron Victor Adlerkreutz, that lug she's been married to, has just been killed in what is described as a shooting accident in the Galloping Domino, a gambling resort about two miles from you, and you're to get on that case at once. It so happens that we're on that risk to the tune of one hundred thousand bucks, every cent of it payable to Sylvia Shoreham, and every cent of it due on a verdict of accident. Layton, when a man gets killed less than one year after taking out a thirty-thousand-dollar straight life policy, less than nine months after taking out a twenty-thousand-dollar endowment policy, and less than six months after taking out a fifty-thousand-dollar accident-and-health policy, it *can't* be on the *up-and-up!* Layton, I don't make any charges against the wife, but I say the beneficiary under these policies is automatically under suspicion! I don't say she killed this man! I don't say anything. But I'm telling you it's worth one hundred thousand dollars to Southwest General that she doesn't get away with any false claims! You're to see that every bit of evidence we're entitled to is put in the record, that the District Attorney is advised of the existence of these policies, that we get a special autopsy, and above all else that she be held and that the body be held until I arrive there. Have you got all that?"

"I have, sir."

"This means one hundred thousand dollars!"

"I understand, sir."

"I'll be there as soon as I get plane space."

"I'll be expecting you, sir."

75

He hung up looking a little less aggressive than he had looked when he first shouted "Contact!" Miss Jennifer, who had kept her key up during the first part of the conversation, had scooted down the street, and now came back with a newspaper. It had the accident all over its front page, with Sylvia's picture prominently displayed, Vicki's a little smaller, and Dmitri's a tiny thing, but recognizable. Mr. Layton read, and Miss Jennifer read over his shoulder, making quick little inquiries to which he made rather uncomfortable replies. Soon she burst out: "Well of all the nerve!"

"No, Gans is right. She—"

"Sylvia Shoreham? Kill somebody? For a measly hundred thousand bucks? Why I bet she makes that on one picture. And besides what *for*? She *had* her divorce. She—"

"We're entitled to an investigation."

"You're entitled to plenty of trouble if you go around accusing *her* of murder. Just because he sees an easy way to get out of paying her, that don't say you've got to go and put your foot in it. You've got to live in this town, he hasn't. And besides, who says you're a claim agent? The last I heard of it you were a salesman, and—"

"I'm head of this agency."

He said this with a certain amount of importance, but in fact it was the crux of the situation that now involved him. It was just a small, one-man agency, having no claim adjusters or special functionaries. As in this city it dealt mainly in life insurance, claims had usually been a simple matter, with Mr. Layton calling personally on the relict, bringing check and often coming away with an application for annuity. That he now, in connection with policies he had never seen, as a result of a case that had broken with the unexpectedness of a cloudburst, should have to discharge ties that he had never once thought about, appealed somewhat to his vanity, but at the same time left a vacant feeling in the pit of his stomach.

Within an hour, the vacant feeling had grown to a dreadful, vacuum-like ache. Treading wholly unfamiliar ground, carefully maintaining an outer show of on-the-job-ness, make-it-short-ism, and close-the-deal-ation, he called first at police headquarters and was shown into the office of Inspector Britten, who was immersed in a detective story and didn't look up at his inquiry as to the status of the Shoreham case. "Why, we're not handling it except for routine help, lab work and stuff like that.

It's a county case, so it's in the hands of the Sheriff."

"You don't know what they've turned up?"

"I don't know a thing, buddy."

Walking over to the courthouse, he entered the Sheriff's office, only to find that the Sheriff was out, and that the Chief Deputy "wouldn't be in a position to make a statement about the case, as it's entirely in Sheriff Lucas's hands."

At the State's Attorney's office, he fared, at first anyway, a little better. As he had information, he was admitted to see Mr. Pease, the county prosecutor. That gentleman listened to the news of the three big policies, nodded, made a note. "Thanks very much, Mr. Layton. If we want further information from you, we'll let you know."

"What do I do about an autopsy?"

"I suppose the police are doing an autopsy, and if you'll show them your credentials they'll let you see their report."

"I mean a special autopsy."

"Have to get a court order for that."

Mr. Layton, who had no idea how to get a court order, or even a very clear idea what a court order was, said quickly: "I see." Then, drawing a deep breath, he said: "Oh, and one other thing, Mr. Pease. We're greatly concerned that she be held, and that the body be held, until the arrival of our representative from Los Angeles, Mr. Gans, and—"

"That *who* be held?"

"The beneficiary under these policies, Miss Shoreham."

"Are you crazy?"

"Well, I was instructed to—"

"You ever been on a case like this before?"

"No sir, not, exactly, but—"

"Then you'd better understand that neither you, nor Mr. Gans, nor the Southwest General, or any other corporation, insurance or otherwise, is telling this state whom to hold or whom not to hold or when to release a body. It would be very convenient for your company, no doubt, to escape payment under its policies by hanging something on Miss Shoreham, as anything they hung on her would probably relieve them of liability. But we're not holding her, or the body, or anybody simply to accommodate you, or help your company beat a hundred-thousand-dollar rap. My suggestion to you and your special representative, Mr. Gans, is that you go a little slow in this case. A hundred thousand dollars probably looks pretty important to you, and I suppose to Mr. Gans. But I doubt if it does to her. Her reputation, though, might be a different matter, and you may find yourself in very serious trouble if you go around making wild charges against her."

"I wasn't making charges. I just—"

"You want her held?"

"Well yes sir, but only—"

"To be held she's got to be charged."

Shriveled, Mr. Layton went out to a drugstore and called his office, only to find that Mr. Gans had left on the three o'clock plane, and directed that hotel reservation be made for him. Mr. Layton didn't walk over to the hotel. He slunk there. At the desk he made a reservation for C. C. Gans, Los Angeles, for one night and possibly two, single room and bath, and O. K.'d the price: $6. But before he could do this he had to wait, while the clerk held colloquy with a girl. She was a rather pretty girl, with bright black eyes, round chubby face, and trim little figure. She was pleasantly dressed, in a little spring suit, and might have been a secretary, except that she had some slight touch of the gangster's moll about her that secretaries don't commonly have. The clerk was quite annoyed by her. "For the tenth time, Miss,

Miss Shoreham is not seeing visitors. I can't ring her phone. She's taking no calls except from the Sheriff's office in case they find her sister, or from the sister herself, in case she calls. Now do I make this clear? You don't seem to get it through your head that a terrible thing happened to her today. Every picture critic, movie reporter, fan magazine, City editor, and just plain fool in five states is trying to get through to her; they've already begun arriving in town hoping to see her in person, and she simply can't see every fan that shows up here and wants to be sent up."

"I'm not a fan. I got business with her."

"Your business will have to wait."

"She might not think so."

"I only go by her instructions."

The girl went off, but didn't leave the hotel. She went to a far corner of the lobby and sat down, to the clerk's obvious annoyance. Mr. Layton finished his business and started to leave, but something in the girl's voice lingered in his ear. It seemed to him that in that "She might not think so" there was some hint of a threat. He turned, crossed to where she sat in a mulish sulk, and said: "I couldn't help hearing what was said to you just now. I wonder if there's

81

something I could do for you? I sometimes transact business for Miss Shoreham."

Insurance was certainly some sort of business, and if he wasn't doing much *transacting* he was at least trying to. She looked him over suspiciously and said: "You a friend hers?"

"Well—more like an agent."

Smiling, as though it had all been settled now he said: "Let's go have some coffee. In the dining room we won't be overheard."

They went into the dining room, ordered coffee and canapes, lit cigarettes. He said: "Nice girl Sylvia. Very nice girl indeed. But she's in one bad mess now."

"What do you mean, bad mess?"

"Don't believe everything you see in the papers."

This cryptic fly, cast at random in the direction of something that might be water and might be a whirl of gnats in Mr. Gans' fevered imagination, brought a flash of fins and a spurt of foam. She said: "So you was in on the dirty work too, hey?"

". . . What dirty work do you mean?"

"At the Domino."

"I was in town."

"You seem to know about it."

"You mean making something look like nothing?"

"That's what I mean."

"Let's say I'm a pretty good guesser."

He laughed. She laughed. She had big white teeth. He remarked on them, and on her eyes, asked if she had Spanish blood. She said no, but she was one eighth Indian. He said he always said if a woman really wanted to be good-looking, one thing she couldn't do without was a drop of Indian blood. He said he ought to have known it, because she had such beautiful black hair. The canapes came, and he poured her coffee, gallantly giving her his sugar. She said it didn't look like there was much use trying to kid him, did it? He said he hoped her eyes weren't kidding him, anyway. Abruptly she said: "I seen something out there today."

"At the Domino?"

"I work there."

"In the bar?"

"I deal blackjack."

"Oh yes of course."

"What's your name?"

"Layton. George M. Layton. What's yours?"

"Call me Ethel."

"Want to call me George?"

"I don't mind. George, I seen it all. I don't mean what they *said* happened. I don't mean what they done to fix it up and make it look like an accident. I mean I *seen* it. But don't get me wrong. I didn't come down here to make her feel bad or anything like that. That's why that clerk made me so sore. I came down here for just the opposite. I came down here to let her know it was all right and she didn't have nothing to fear. I come down to let her know that so far as I was concerned that husband of hers was a heel. You'd be that amazed, George, if you knew the propositions he made me, while I was dealing him blackjack not an hour before she shot him. Wanted me to drive back to his shack with him for a 'small fun,' he kept calling it. Can you imagine that? It's not any of my business what was done. Just the same I do think she ought to make it worth my while. Don't you think that's only right?"

"I do indeed."

"You'd think she'd *want* to do something like that."

"I guarantee she wants to."

"So if you want to take me up there—"

"Not so fast, not so fast. Taking you up there would be simple, some other time, but, as you can easily imagine, she's got her own reasons for not seeing anybody today, not even me. Don't worry though, it'll be handled. Does she *know* you saw it? Were you there?"

"In the door there's a slot, with bars in front and a steel door behind. The door was open a little bit. I peeped in."

"And you saw something, is that it?"

"I seen him killed."

"By her?"

"If I told you that, you'd know as much as I do, wouldn't you? Suppose you do some talking now. And talk nice. About money."

"To spill it or skip it?"

"To skip it, I would rather imagine."

"She'll be interested to hear that."

"What do I do now?"

"Let me think. Where's Spiro?"

"Out at the Domino."

"I think he's the guy, not Shoreham."

"I would have gone to him, but he and Tony are so thick all of a sudden I was afraid. I work for Tony and I didn't know how he'd take it."

"I'm awfully glad you came here first. Now here's what you do. Have a buck off me and see yourself a nice picture. Around seven o'clock or so, come back here and wait to be paged. Don't go back to the Domino till you hear from me."

When Mr. Layton entered the Domino, Tony was being pointedly disagreeable to some schoolgirls, telling them Miss Shoreham was not there, that he had no idea when she might come there, and that they certainly could not leave their autograph books for her to sign. It didn't seem a propitious time for inquiry, so Mr. Layton bought $1 worth of 10¢ chips and began playing roulette, but soon the phone girl came through, her plug bouncing against her knees calling his name. Tony said he might take the call in the office. It was Miss Jennifer, whom he had informed of his movements, with a telegram from Mr. Gans, evidently his last testament before explaining. It was full of exhortations like: *"Cannot impress on you too strongly importance prompt energetic aggressive action your part or refrain calling your attention Southwest General will expect some cooperation you she expects gets every man her organization."*

Mr. Layton listened as Miss Jennifer read this to him over the phone, then, two or three times, he heard something that was quite familiar to him, on account of Miss Jennifer's habits. It was the sound of a key being lifted. As he hung up, a short, round, flat-headed little man came into the office, and began peering at a road map that hung on the wall. Suddenly, fitting Tony's surprising courtesy, the key, and the little man together, Mr. Layton knew this call had been tapped, and he felt a hot, salt taste in his mouth, for he needed nobody to tell him that the pure in heart do not plug in on other people's lines.

Thus he who had been paralyzed by officialdom, by ignorance of the ropes he was trying to handle, by a conviction that he was afoot on an absurd and monstrous errand, had now become a different man, and an incomparably dangerous one. For bland cheek was an integral part of his daily life; he not only had a gift for it, but believed in it, as the sign of an up-and-at-'em-tude, and studied it avidly under the district manager, other agents, and such experts in salesmanship. He was a virtuoso at keeping the other fellow guessing, at never giving him a chance to take charge of the interview, of feinting him into the path of the argument held in reserve. He could dissemble, he could laugh, he could tell a little joke. He could be stern, he could plead. He could wink. And he could defeat, by stratagems developed by the whole inner arcanum of insurance agents, any known method of throwing him out.

He didn't address Dmitri at once; indeed, he didn't seem to pay any attention to Dmitri. Instead, he drummed on the desk with annoyed finger tips, then lifted the receiver and asked for a number. When it answered he said: "Sheriff Lucas, please—Layton calling, George Layton of Southwest General . . . Well listen, sweetie, I don't like to get disagreeable about it, but haven't you any idea at all where he is, or when he'll be in, or how I can get hold of him? . . . No, there's no way *he* can reach *me*. I'll be on the move all afternoon and there's no use having him call . . . I'm sorry too, and I suppose you're doing your best and that God loves you or somebody does, but you're putting me to one awful lot of unnecessary trouble."

Hanging up, he spoke with the baffled weariness of one who has puzzled over human nature all his life, but can still make no sense out of it: "Maybe you can figure this one out. Sheriff Parker Lucas. If there's been any time in the last two years when you couldn't see that long-legged jerk anywhere you went, with his hand out for a cigar, a drink, a phone number, or what have you, I don't know when it could it been. But now, on a murder case, when I want him, when

I'd like something for my vote, try and find him. It's a great life if you like a great life. Personally, I'd rather see a picture."

On the word *murder,* which was the only part of this elaborate harangue that mattered, he saw Dmitri's eyes leave the map and stare glassily at the wall. He lifted the phone, rang Miss Jennifer again, asked airily if the Sheriff had called. Then he went out, paid the operator for his calls. Then he went in the gentlemen's room, combed his hair, whistled The Minstrel Boy. When he came out, Tony and Dmitri were in a corner of the casino, whispering. He went into the office, called the apartment where he lived, and where he knew there would be nobody. He was holding the receiver to his ear, frowning at getting no answer, when Dmitri came into the room and went to the map again. But he looked up pleasantly when Dmitri said: "You been to Goldfield?"

"Oh yeah, plenty of times."

"They have a hotel there, yes?"

"The old brick hotel, it's still there. Little more hotel than Goldfield needs right now, but they'll take care of you."

"Always wanted to see this place. *Doch,* it's impossible to start now. I want to see the

Sharf, too. What makes you think it's a murder case?"

"Think? I know."

"You talked to the police, yes?"

"Yeah, I talked to them, but I generally always haven't got time to wait for the police to wake up. Insurance is my line. Southwest General of N. A., and when you've handled as many cases as I have, you know and you don't even know how you know. You just smell it."

"I don't smell nothing, myself."

"To me, it's quite a stink."

There was a long pause, while Mr. Layton set his heels on the desk and lit a cigar. When he could see through the wreathing smoke, he noted that Tony was in the room. Then, with the air of one who regretfully pronounces a final judgment on matter long since closed, he said: "Her big mistake was making it accident. That gets an insurance company a little sore. Now if he was just dead, then O. K., he had to die sometime, and we were on the risk. But when she made it accident, that made a big accident-and-health bond operative, and that makes a difference of fifty thousand bucks. Well, that's just too bad."

". . . *She?* Who are you talking about?"

"Shoreham. The widow."

"You mean *she* made it accident?"

"She gets the dough, don't she? As beneficiary?"

"How can you talk that way?"

"What have you got to do with it?"

Mr. Layton snapped this at Dmitri sharply, as though his discussing the case at all were a very suspicious circumstance. But Dmitri looked at Mr. Layton as though he were plain crazy. "You ask me that? What I have to do with? Me? Dmitri Spiro, president of Phoenix Pictures, that makes all Shoreham production? Me, the best friend of Baron Adlerkreutz? You ask me what *I* have to do with it?"

"And what have *you* got to do with it?"

Tony was cold, hard, malevolent. Mr. Layton answered with a smile, a genial freckled smile, in the accents of Dmitri. "Me? You ask me what I got to do with it? Me, agency chief for Southwest General of N. A.?" Then, speaking with a smile not so genial, he asked Tony: *"And what have you got to do with it?"*

"You can go to prison in this state. For slander."

"And you could hang for murder."

"Suppose you get out."

91

"O. K., O. K."

He got up, but Dmitri held up his hand, said there should be no hard feelings, that Tony didn't really mean what he said. Mr. Layton, turning from the door in very friendly fashion, said; "Yes sir, yes sir, making it accident was bad. If it had been suicide, now, I wouldn't have a word to say."

Tony and Dmitri looked at each other, and Dmitri said: "Why?"

"We don't pay off on suicide. Not for three years, we don't. It used to be one year, but during the depression we raised it. Got to be too many fellows taking out a fifty-thousand-dollar life policy in favor of the little woman, then diving out a fifteenth-story window in some hotel downtown. Same way on the accident-and-health, all bets off on suicide. So, if she'd made it suicide, it wouldn't have concerned the Southwest General of N. A. even a little bit. But when she made it accident, that concerns us a lot. That means exactly one hundred thousand bucks to us, so it's what you might call, the hundred-thousand-dollar mistake. I'm going to miss her, too. I go to all her pictures. All of them."

He sat down again, in no hurry to go. Dmitri stared at Tony in abject misery, and

Tony stared at Mr. Layton, a look in his eye that one sees in the eye of a Siberian tiger. After a long time, Dmitri looked over and said: "Look here, old man. It's ridiculous. It's quite ridiculous. It was an accident, we all know it was an accident. I was there. He died in my arms. Just the same, nobody wants any trouble. Can't we make a deal? Can't—"

"*Hey, hey, hey!*" Mr. Layton jumped up as though he had been shot, and said: "Don't you talked to me about any deal. *Not to me!*"

"Why not?" Tony's tone was savage.

"Weren't you talking about laws?"

"Laws? What do you care about laws? All you're thinking about is money. O. K., so it's dead open-and-shut. Why don't you make a deal? It's like Mr. Spiro says, you're talking through your hat, there's been no crime. But she's a big picture actress and your measly hundred grand don't mean half as much to her as not having any mess. Well, suppose they agree to tear up your policies? What do you care? Don't that let you out?"

Mr. Layton had a wild, instinctive notion that Mr. Gans, if he had been present, would have made a deal. But he had got a great deal further than he had even dreamed was possible, and his only clear idea was that he had to get out of there, that he had no authority to make a deal, that he had to consult Mr. Gans. Then, probably a deal would still be possible. Blandly he asked Tony: "Where's Ethel?"

"What's Ethel got to do with it?"

"Ethel saw something today."

"Such as, what?"

"I don't exactly know. Mighty pretty girl, Ethel is. Part Indian."

Tony's pasty pallor, as well as Dmitri's soft look of complete collapse, told him quite a lot. Mr Layton added: "She's not coming back to work, I guess. She's a little worried, though I can't imagine what for." Then, to Spiro, "I'd talk to Ethel, if I were you. She'll be in the lobby of Shoreham's hotel at seven o'clock."

He picked up his hat, and there was a tense, strained silence. A tall man and a thin man came in, pitched a package of telegrams and letters on the desk. The tall man said: "Fan stuff mostly, been coming in at the hotel ever since the story went on the air. I told Western Union to hold the rest of it and we'd pick it up. This stuff, I thought, we better take charge of it, so nothing gets lost."

94

"O. K., Bushy. Thanks."

Benny sat nervously down. Mr. La Bouche suddenly said "Oh," as though he had just remembered something, and found a letter in the stack of telegrams. Leaning close he mumbled: "It's that special Vicki sent her, in case she wouldn't answer his call. I took it along, because God knows how it'll affect her. Better hang onto it a few days, hah? Before we give it to her to read?"

Dmitri fingered the letter, stared at the special delivery stamp, at the round clock with an arrow showing the time of receipt, that had been stamped by the hotel. Then, looking straight at Mr. Layton, he said: "Boys, I got an awful premonition creeping up my back that in this communication Victor Adlerkreutz announces his intention to take his own life."

"What?"

Benny's mouth hung open in amazement, but Mr. La Bouche grabbed him quickly and said: "Shut up! I would think you'd know by now that when Mr. Spiro has something creeping up his back, he's practically never wrong."

But Mr. Layton, so badly crossed up he didn't quite know what he was doing, was already at the door. To Dmitri he said: "I'm going. If that's a suicide note, I know you don't want any strangers around when you read it." Then, not sure that he shouldn't make some show of encouragement, he turned a ghastly smile at Dmitri and said; "Yeah, I know you're kind of unstrung about it."

Promptly at 5:30, Mr. Gans came up the ramp, his jaw stuck out and his lower teeth visible against his lip. He listened to what Mr. Layton had to say, made no comment until they were almost in the center of town. Then, with explosive vehemence, he said: "Great! You've done the right thing, Layton! You've used your head and you've used your guts and Southwest General of N. A. is proud, of you! I always say, be aggressive! Move fast! But, if the other party listens to reason, be reasonable! After all what are we, Layton? Insurance men, not hangmen!"

Chapter Eight

Mr. Layton had barely left the room when Tony leaped at Dmitri, caught him by the arm and began shaking him savagely. "Are you nuts? Listen fellow, you can't trifle with

96

this thing! What'll they think of us, cooking up a dilly like we told them already, and then saying it isn't so? Spiro, you dealt these cards, and there's no way now to make it a misdeal! You've got to play them!"

"Didn't you hear what he said?"

"Couldn't you make a deal?"

"Didn't you hear me try? What happened?"

"Couldn't you sock him in the jaw?"

"*Me?* He was a big guy. *You* sock him."

"Taking it lying down—"

"Wait a minute, fellow—wait a minute. This wasn't just a guy. He was from a big insurance company. What good would it do to sock him?"

"It would do plenty of good. A cheap jack of an agent comes out here, lights a cigar, and scares you so bad you turn around and pitch it all out, what's been done. Don't you get it? *I'm* in on it too! I've been your witness, I've stood for what had to be said to put across accident. Look where that puts me in this town if you go around and tell them it's all just a lie you thought up."

Mr. La Bouche spoke in a quiet, worried way. "We think we been getting away with it, but who says we have? Who says that mug is from an insurance company at all? Who says he's not a cop stool pigeon?"

"But switching, that'll fix it, hey?"

They all sat in gloom for a few minutes. Then Dmitri picked up the letter. "And besides this note can't go to the Sheriff. It must be another note. Because who knows what this says? Maybe some fool thing. Maybe something about Hezzel. Maybe cracks it wide open."

"Can't you *burn* it?"

Mr. La Bouche explained patiently to Tony that if it had been merely an ordinary letter, burning was possible, but with the post office having a record of the delivery, to say nothing of the hotel, burning would be wholly risky. Substituting another letter, one that indicated Vicki intended to take his own life, was the best solution all around. And Dmitri added: "We don't switch, nothing like that. We tell the same thing. Just like we told it before. Except we remember now, it was Vicki who say, 'I must have a real one.' Was *Vicki* who say, 'I don't get this thing till you make it plain.' We know nothing about a note. The *Sharf* opens the note, says it must be suicide. Then all see it was suicide, the insurance goes *kaput*, company no have to pay."

Tony stormed, pleaded, called Dmitri names. But Benny, the first forger of his time, went out, and when he returned he had the bar's small electric coffee machine. Filling it with water from the cooler he plugged it in, and while he was waiting for it to steam he looked at the letter. "Green ink, pals. That's the first thing. Where's his pen? Anything you put inside has to match up with this envelope outside, if I'm doing it — if the idea is, we're using this envelope. I guess that's what you mean, use the envelope to show it come in to the hotel before he even got shot."

Mr. Spiro unclipped a pen from his shirt pocket, handed it over. "He borrowed *my* pen to write it with. All full up, all full up with green ink."

Benny turned the letter over. "Worse and more of it. Maybe the wop is right. Maybe we better leave it lay. Because the flap has a crown on it. It has that crown on it, and the inside paper will have to match."

"That's under control."

Mr. La Bouche explained that he and Dmitri both knew where Vicki kept his paper, up at the shack and that they would get some at once. This proved to be unduly optimistic, for their entrance into the shack was barred by officers at the door; but on their plea of checking what clothes would be needed for the funeral they were let in, and under the guise of making memoranda they helped themselves to paper, and were back at the Domino in less than an hour. By that time, Benny had steamed open the envelope, extracted the brief note that it contained and tabulated the words in it, in pencil, on another sheet of paper. He pointed the pencil at Mr. La Bouche and Dmitri, looking very solemn. "Now get this, lugs. This presents one of the most unusual problems I ever had challenge me professional skill. How this guy spelled the English language was something to write home about. He had his own system, but it was nothing like Webster's system, or anybody's system. But this is what it means: You got to say what you say with these specimen words, these words I got wrote out here, that he used in the original note. Because that's all the words I can be sure of. Because if I go and spell a word one way, and they dig up a lot of his handwriting at the shack and compare, and he spelled it some other way, that cooks us, friends. You got it?"

Tony scowled, but whether Dmitri or Mr. La Bouche heard it, would be hard to say.

They were walking abstractedly about, passing and repassing each other on the linoleum carpet, in the throes of literary composition. Presently Mr. La Bouche said: "There ought to be an affectionate note in it, Dimmy. That's what I miss in all this. Nobody seems to *care.*"

"Like for instance, Bushy, how do you mean?"

"Well, you know, something like 'My mind is all on you, Sylvia,' or maybe 'My heart is all *with* you' would be better, 'as the shadows lengthen toward the west.' "

"East."

"East. Right. You got that, Benny?"

"Look, get this once and for all. If any shadows lengthen in this, they lengthen toward the north, because that was where he was going on his honeymoon and its the only point on the compass I know how he spelled it. He didn't bother with any H, but how do I know he didn't spell east with a Y? Maybe he thought it was rich in vitamins."

"Shadows are out."

"Bushy, you see something so: The end of my lang, lang trail a-winding? Course that's not it, but it gives a rough idea. I wan' something with a punch."

"Boys, something short would help."

"The Long, Long Trail is in."

"Trip with two P's, but no trail. Sorry."

"And then, Dimmy, of course I'm only spitballing throw it out if you don't like it. But don't you think there ought to be some *little* thing? Like, 'Be kind to—' What was the name of that hyena he had in the private zoo out on the ranch?"

"You can have 'switt puss,' but no hyena."

"Maybe he's right. The hyena's name was Spiro."

"Dimmy, on a thing like this I always like a quotation of some kind. We'll say like a question from Shakespeare."

"On that, Bushy, I would hesitate."

"It would give it class."

"But suppose they find out how Vicki felt about Shakespeare? After Julius Caesar flopped, Vicki always said Shakespeare was lousy."

"There might be two opinions about that."

"I know. I know how Vicki came to produce Julius Caesar. He was wishing he didn't have to pay for a script and somebody told him about Shakespeare, and he said 'Why not? It don't cost anything to find out.' So we made it and it flopped, and it cost more than the Phoenix Studios cost. Just the same, he blamed it on Shakespeare, and I don't know if we should put it from Shakespeare."

They volleyed the point back and forth, while the shadow of the Sierras crept closer, and presently enveloped the Domino in luminous blue. Benny, the pencil clicking against his teeth, studied the limited vocabulary which must form the basis of the projected composition, and presently started to write first in pencil on scratch paper, then with the fountain pen on Vicki's crested stationery. Soon talk ceased and an uneasy silence fell on the room. He wrote slowly, trying every word on the scratch paper, smoking and considering. He must have been under a strain, for when Dmitri complained at the rate of progress, he snapped back: "Shut up and lemme alone. To do justice to me skill I got to take me time." When the note was done he handed it over, first reminding them to handle it with handkerchiefs. Though Tony refused even to look, Dmitri and Mr. La Bouche read the following:

Dienstag

Silvya, Switt Puss, Kuss Kuss: Be oder not be, that is quashon. Today-huete comes Divarse-peper, todayheute comes And. Silvya Puss, I can no live

wit out You. My Son go don, nort
Star come opp, is batter Vicki go out.
So, Gottbei. Gottbei Dimmy, Gottbei
Buschka, Gottbei, Gott hehute
Hezelchen. Wiedersehen & Kuss Kuss.

Dein

Vicki

Be gut gegen "Spiro."

Chapter Nine

The Sheriff spent a solitary afternoon on
the front porch of his home, which was a
pleasant house in the middle of a ranch four
or five miles from town, on a road that
forked off the road that led past the Galloping Domino. It was a cattle ranch, and he
sat staring at his beeves; as to what was going
on in his mind his face gave no clue. Once
he went inside, picked up the phone that
stood on a small table in the hall and called
Mr. Flynn, to see if anything had been heard
of the missing girl. Once Mr. Flynn called
him, to say that there was such a jam of calls
from the special writers who were arriving
by plane, train, car and bus, that nothing was
coming in from outlying parts of the state

at all. The Sheriff told him to notify the police what he was doing, then lock the office and go out to the Galloping Domino, having all long distance calls transferred to there. Then, if the police learned something, they could report it, while other dial calls would simply get no answer. Mr. Flynn said O. K. The Sheriff, as soon as he had eaten a light supper served him by the Mexican woman who kept house for him, got in his car and drove over there. He found Mr. Flynn in the office, studying a pile of photostats, charts and reports. "What do they show, Flynn?"

"Not a thing."

"All checks up?"

"So far, it does. Only fingerprints on the gun are Spiro's, but the way he tells it he was the one had hold of the barrel, and it's only on the barrel you get clear prints. Trajectory of the bullet corresponds right. Fired from an angle, on the right, which would just about be the way it would be doing the scene the way they said they did it. I don't see anything wrong with it. What do you want the girl for?"

"Sister's worried about her."

"When are you having the inquest?"

"Soon as we find her. Did you eat?"

"Not yet I haven't."

"You better go, then. I'll sit in here and take anything that comes along. Take your time. I'm not going anywhere."

When Mr. Flynn had gone, the Sheriff dug into the pile of evidential matter a bit grimly, and perhaps more carefully than Mr. Flynn had done. Soon the door opened and Dmitri came in. He said: "He told you, Sharf? Mr. Flynn? About this stuff?"

"What stuff?"

Dmitri pointed to a stack of communications brought from the hotel, explained why they had not been given to Sylvia. The Sheriff said: "O. K. I'll release them to you after the inquest."

"This one note—"

"Yes?"

"It's from Vicki. I can tell by the crest. He borrowed my pen last night to write her a note. I didn't give it to her yet. Might make her feel bad."

The Sheriff picked up the note, dropped it in his pocket, went back to his photostats. Dmitri said: "You're not reading it?"

"It's to her, isn't it?"

"I thought maybe, was evidence."

"Of what?"

"Skip, skip."

"You did right in turning it over to me,

106

and I'll see that she gets it. Now, is there anything else you wanted to see me about?"

"No, sir. No, thanks. You want me, I'll be at Sylvia's hotel at seven o'clock."

"O. K."

Dmitri had barely gone when a call came, and the Sheriff answered. "Officer Enders talking from Lone Pine."

"Sheriff Lucas. What is it, Enders?"

"We found her."

"Alive?"

"No,"

"That's what I expected. Shoot."

"The Army planes reported it, right after dark. Two lights pointed straight up at the sky. They took it for some kind of signal at first, and we got over there. The car was standing on its rear bumper, jammed against a ledge. It couldn't be seen from the road. She must have driven it over on purpose, because there was no way it could have swerved that far by accident.

"What have you done with the body?"

"Nothing. Waiting orders."

"You have an ambulance there?"

"Yes, sir. Called one before I climbed down there."

"Then send her right in to town. No inquest necessary, that I see. Come in yourself and report to me here at the Galloping Domino at nine thirty. I'll call the Adlerkreutz inquest for ten."

"Yes, sir. Is Flynny there?"

"He's at supper."

"I got one on him. I turned up more dirt on the other one, the sister Sylvia, that picture actress he was bragging about.

"You—did what?"

"Didn't he tell you?"

"No."

"He met her today. She shook hands with him, or so he says. Boy, was he letting me know it. Well, it just so happens that when we went looking for Hazel, we turned up a trail on Sylvia that would make a hooker in the Red Mill at Tijuana look like a Minnesota schoolteacher. If there's any tinhorn sport in this state she hasn't checked in with at some hotel the last two months, I don't know who he could be. Tell Flynny we found another one: Mrs. John L. Smith, registered at Bill's Place, six miles below here, exactly one month ago today; except that Mrs. Smith, when somebody went up and asked her to autograph the lunchroom menu, signed it

Sylvia Shoreham. Will you tell him, Sheriff? I just love to rib Flynny."

"I sure will."

"Thanks, Sheriff."

When Mr. Flynn returned, the Sheriff said; "Is this all the stuff you got?"

"That's all. This outer stuff, the picture people brought it from the hotel, but I couldn't see what we had to do with it. I didn't even open it."

"Where's the report from Enders?"

"From—*who* did you say?"

"Enders. At Lone Pine."

"That wasn't a report. That was a rib."

"What he told me was a report."

"Then write it up."

"It was a report and you wrote it and where is it?"

Mr. Flynn hesitated for a moment, said nothing. He was a big, heavy-set man of forty, darkly sunburned, vividly handsome in his slacks and flannel shirt. Presently he said: "What's the big idea, Parker? You've been stuck on this woman four or five years now, and I don't blame you. She shook hands with me this morning, and when she came out she remembered my name, and when I rang her a little while ago to tell her how we were coming, she still remembered it. She's a swell girl. Well, so she's been playing around? Well, so what? What have you got to do with that?"

"I'm asking you for Enders' report."

His face purpling deeply under its sunburn, Mr. Flynn went behind the desk, opened the center drawer. In it was a little pile of scratch-pad sheets, with penciled memoranda on them. He found the one he wanted, handed it to the Sheriff. "O. K. she registered at these three hotels on these three dates under these three names, the men she was with all different. She was seen by several different people at each place and didn't even try to conceal who she was. There you are. That's the Enders report."

"Are those other officers' reports?"

". . . Yes."

"Hand them over."

Sylvia, like most actresses, had made an art of relaxation: it held the secret of bright eyes, glowing color, and the vivacity needed in front of a camera. She lay on her bed now, eyes closed, hands folded on her stomach, no part of her moving except her chest, which rose and fell a little as she breathed. She had put on a black dress, but even without this she would have looked pale, haggard, and worn

110

in the half light that came in from the street, for it had been in truth a trying day. But she was not asleep, for an alert hand went out at the first sound of the phone: she had given orders that she was to be disturbed for two calls only: her sister, or the Sheriff. The desk informed her that the Sheriff was in the lobby. She jumped up, put on her shoes, patted her face, and went out to admit her guest.

He came in, and at her invitation sat down on the hotel sofa, not answering her question about her sister. She turned on the lights she wanted, poked up the fire the hotel had made for her. Then she went over, sat down beside him and contentedly put her head on his shoulder. "Is there any news?"

He said nothing, and his arm did not go around her. After a long time he said: "Yes." His voice had hanging fur on it, and shook. For the first time she really looked at him then, and became aware of his eyes. They hadn't softened since they sobered Mr. Flynn, and by now, indeed, were a little frightening. He waited a long time before he went on, in slow, husky, measured words: "This morning, after saying you killed a man, you told me you thought you did right. I couldn't hardly believe my ears then. I've killed two men since I held this office, and I never felt I did right. I felt I did what I had to, but I hated it. Now I know what you meant. Because I could kill you, as I sit here right now, and I wouldn't feel it was wrong. I'd feel it was right."

"And why do I deserve to die?"

"Because you've been deceiving me, and the people of this country, and the people of the whole world. Because you're not what you pretend to be. Because you're living a dirty, rotten lie."

"I don't know what you're talking about."

From his pocket he took a wad of crumpled scratch-pad sheets. Smoothing out the first one, he studied it and said: "On March 8, you spent the day at the Tumble Inn Roadhouse thirty miles south of here with a man that was known to several people there as Ted Genesee, a croupier, at the Luckbuck Club not two blocks from here. You signed in as Mr. and Mrs. Edward Gentile, you spent the day, and at five o'clock he drove you back here. On April 2 you spent another day with Genesee at the Garden motor court, on the road east. On April 3 you didn't bother to leave town, but checked in with him at the Westhaven, down at the depot. On April 5 you switched off from Genesee to a Cuban named Carlos Loma, that handles the stick for Dawson's crap game over at the Monte Carlo. You went with him to Bill's Place, down the line, and Hollister's Dude Ranch, and Hack Schultz's camp up in the mountains."

He laid aside the first slip and picked up the second. He talked for ten minutes, giving names, dates and places, and when he got through he was twisting his face, and occasionally squeezing his mouth with his hand, to keep from sobbing. When he had some sort of control he burst out: "How could you come over to me this morning with all that talk about hating those cheap pictures and tell me you were going to make more like The Glory of Edith Cavell? And how could you pretend to be Edith Cavell?"

"I didn't pretend to be Edith Cavell."

"You did."

"I was an actress playing a part."

"You used her name and said her words and died her death and for two hours you pretended to be her. And all that time you were nothing but a common trollop that anybody could have, and if I were to go out of here and leave you dead on the floor right now, it wouldn't be any more than you deserve, or any different from how women like you generally wind up."

She started several times to say something, each time swallowed it back. Then she sat with a fixed desperate look on her face, staring into the fire. He said: "You told me this morning you killed your husband."

"I did kill him."

"I don't believe you."

"A jury will, I think."

"Do you want them to?"

"Dimmy says it was an accident, and so will I."

"Your sister killed your husband."

"No! No!"

"I say she did. If he said he would marry her and then he wouldn't do it, that would be enough reason for a whole lot of women, You didn't have any reason."

"I told you it was the only way out."

"Except to sign his contract."

"Will you sign a confession you did it?"

". . . Yes."

"Then you better write it. Because I'm telling you, I know who did it."

After a long time she got up, went over to the writing desk and wrote:

To Whom It May Concern:

Today, at approximately 12:30 P.M., at the Galloping Domino Gambling Hall, I shot and killed my husband, Victor Adlerkreutz. My sister, Hazel Shoreham, was not present, but will probably say she did it in order to save me. This will not be true.

Sylvia Shoreham

She got up, handed it to him, and resumed her seat on the sofa, He went over to the desk, put it in an envelope, marked it "Shoreham Confession." Then he said: "This ends the matter."

"Am I under arrest?"

"Your sister has been found."

"She—where is she?"

"It's bad news."

Briefly, under terrible emotion, he told her what had happened. Then he said: "Sylvia Shoreham, I love you more than any human being on earth. I'd give my right arm to be able to touch you right now. I'd give the other arm if I could be the one that helped you through this sorrow that must be heavy to you, I know how heavy from the way you've tried to protect that girl. But I don't forget that judge, in the picture. He knew that woman hadn't done what she said she did, but he did what he thought he had to do just the same. That girl can't ever be tried for her crime now. She's beyond human justice, and she's beyond speaking for you, too. I've called an inquest at ten o'clock tonight, and at that inquest I'm going to let Spiro and his friends make it accident. I'll let you bury the dead, and have no more trouble about it. But if you try to go into pictures again, I have this and I'll use it. And you can tell Spiro that The Glory of Edith Cavell goes back in the can and it stays there. You are not going to pretend to be something you're not any more, if I've got anything to do with it."

Her face didn't move a muscle, and he got up. "Isn't that funny? At that lunch we were going to have, I was going to ask you to start a fund for our tuberculosis hospital. It's a poor state, and we got no hospital and we ought to have one, and it could be built now, for soldier use, and then turned back to us later. That's what I was going to ask."

"I don't mind contributing."

His face was tortured, and his eyes full of tears, "I can't take your money. If I did I'd have to tear up your confession, and

116

I swear that stays with me till I die—or you do."

He looked at the envelope, put it in his pocket. Then, a blank look in his face, he pulled out the other envelope, the one Dmitri had given him. Identifying it after a moment, he said: "This came for you. Spiro didn't give it to you because well, I guess you can guess why."

He laid the envelope in her lap. It was Vicki's Baltic handwriting that did what nothing else had yet done: it brought a torrent of tears, She said: "I can't face it . . . I've had all I can stand today! I—"

He went over, picked up the letter, walked with it to the fireplace, dropped it on the flames. Then his shoulders shaking, he stumbled out of the room.

Chapter Ten

At nine, Mr. Flynn closed the Domino down, and for the next hour quite an assortment of people assembled there. More and more officers showed up, until there were a dozen or more. Most of them brought evidential exhibits of one kind and another, which they left with Mr. Flynn in the office, so the desk was piled high with envelopes of various sizes, all neatly labeled. Then there were the correspondents. Some of them had arrived on the afternoon plane, some by train, some by car, but there were a score or more of them. They were reinforced by several local people who corresponded for picture publications, and who got about one item like this a year and made the most of it. Then there were reporters from the local papers, with their photographers. Then there was Mr. Britten, who sat apart and had little to say to his men. Then there was Mr. Pease, the county prosecutor, who did not as a rule attend inquests, believing that his presence embarrassed the Coroner, but who made an exception of tonight, possibly because of the opportunity that would be presented to shake hands with a prominent actress. Tony, with worried, abstracted politeness, found seats for all: big crowds, after all, were not a new event in his life.

Dmitri arrived around a quarter to ten, with Mr. La Bouche, but not with Benny. Almost on his heels came Mr. Layton, with Mr. Gans and another man who looked like a lawyer. He was a new Mr. Layton, one who had expanded and put on fifty pounds of weight sine the afternoon, a commanding, calm figure of a man who dominated his two companions as a general dominates his aides, and waved them to seats with that kindly thoughtfulness that does not owe courtesy but graciously bestows it. Then he went to a corner and beckoned Dmitri over. When Mr. La Bouche came too, he smiling shook his head, and Mr. La Bouche retired. Dmitri, however, had changed since the afternoon himself. He had stiffened, and reverted to his usual lofty peevishness. He said: "What you want?" in a bellicose way, and then, without waiting for Mr. Layton to speak, added querulously: "Plizze, plizze, my time is waluable."

Mr. Layton said: "What's cooking?"

"What do you mean, cooking?"

"Was that a suicide note in that box today?"

"I don't know. The Sharf took it. You'll have to ask him."

"You see Ethel?"

"What were you doing, trying to kid me? Hinting around that she knew something? She's just a pretty girl that wants little job in pictures. So, I've given her a job. Tomorrow she goes to Hollywood, and tonight she come here. So plizze, am busy man."

119

"Getting tough, hey?"

"Not tough, only busy."

"She didn't like it, how you treated her."

"What did you say?"

"She thought three grand wasn't much for what she knew. She thought considering how much it's worth to you, you didn't take that liberal, friendly attitude she'd been hoping for. She thought you acted in quite a tightwad way, and she's hurt."

"How do you know what she thought?"

"That's not her with Benny."

"What? That went to the picture show. He called me—"

"That's her girl friend. Right now, she's having a ride in my car. She likes my car. She likes me. And she'll be right where I want her when the time comes. However, since you're busy—"

"What do you want, ha?"

"I asked you something."

"You mean this note?"

"Yeah. Start talking."

"I'm pretty sure it's a suicide note. The Sharf, he didn't open the note, when I gave it to him. He took it to give Sylwia, but it should be suicide note."

"Fellow, it better be a suicide note."

"Plizze, plizze. It will be."

"If you had your policies here, so accidentally on purpose they could get burned, it would end my interest in the case. But since you haven't, and the verdict at tonight's inquest is going to determine my liability, I don't take chances. I'm telling: it better be a suicide note."

"Plizze. Wait only."

"Then O. K."

Mr. Layton returned to Mr. Gans and the lawyer. Dmitri went over and stood looking unhappily into a juke-box. Mr. Pease, the prosecutor, drifted over to Mr. Britten. "Cy, did you notice something just now?"

"Not particularly."

"An objectionable party by the name of Layton was in my office this afternoon, representing an insurance company. He wanted a special autopsy and all but demanded I charge Sylvia Shoreham with murder. Now he just went into a huddle with Dmitri Spiro. You know, these insurance companies go too far. I wouldn't ask much to rap that bird over the knuckles for obstructing justice."

"He was in to see me too."

"Oh yeah?"

"I had him followed."

". . . What for?"

"Just a hunch. He had another talk with

Spiro, before this one. Out here at the Domino, for a half hour this afternoon. But before that he met a girl that deals blackjack out here, and then later, after he met his boss at the plane and they got a lawyer over to the hotel, he met the girl again, and they went up to his apartment, and you'll notice she's not here."

"What are you getting at, Cy?"

"Something funny about this case."

"You don't mean it's *my* case?"

"You heard about the sister?"

"I didn't attach much importance to her."

"They found her. Dead."

"What?"

"Couple of hours ago."

"Say, I think I'll stick around."

Sylvia arrived on the stroke of ten, a fur coat over her black dress, a small black hat with veil giving her face a wan, pale look. With her was Dr. Daly, the lawyer who had obtained her divorce. The Sheriff, who had been in the office with Mr. Flynn, the undertaker, and a deputy now came out. It was the deputy's question to the undertaker about shipment of the Shoreham body that informed the correspondents of the second

122

fatality in the case, and at once they crowded around him, asking questions. He put up his hand: "I don't know any more than you do. Shoreham's been to the mortuary and made formal identification of both bodies. Now the Coroner's bringing his jury out here for the inquest. Don't get excited and soon you'll know all that anybody knows."

As he spoke the Coriner arrived, with another deputy shepherding the jury, six unhappy-looking wretches, four men and two women, all middle-aged except one of the men, who looked like a young law student. On their heels came the interne who had responded to the first call and the two orderlies who had come with him, all looking like members of the high school football team. A dozen other men arrived. The Coroner at once took the jury and a number of others into the office, where Mr. Flynn pointed to the spot where the body had been found. The Coroner was evidently hurrying, for he bowed once or twice, in an apologetic sort of way, to Sylvia, and kept saying to his jury: "Just so you get the picture, that's all. We'll put it all in evidence in the regular way, under oath when we examine witnesses, but it'll save time if you look the place over and get it all clear in your minds."

He then led the way back to the casino, where a roulette table had been set in the middle of the floor for his convenience, with chairs for the jury and a single chair as a witness stand. He sat down and Mr. Flynn sat beside him, rapping for order with the croupier's stick and announcing the opening of an inquest into the death of (with a glance at a memorandum he held in his hand) Victor Alexis Olaf Hermann Adlerkreutz, and summoning all who had knowledge of the event to come forward and give their evidence. He then directed witnesses to hold up their right hands, so that they might all be sworn together. Quite a few hands went up, including a number of constabular hands. He then bound them to tell the truth, the whole truth, and nothing but the truth, and the Coroner cleared his throat and called the young interne who had pronounced Vicki dead. He gave his testimony briefly, and the orderlies, on inquiry from the Coroner, said that was how they remembered it. Next was a physician who made the autopsy. He reported with considerable medical verbiage. Then police photographers were called and identified their work. Tony was called. He hadn't witnessed the shooting himself, he said, but he had supplied the gun on Mr. Spiro's plea they wanted to rehearse a picture scene. Mr. La Bouche was next, and repeated what he had said earlier in the day, with gruesome details this time, about how he had been manipulating the imaginary camera, as represented by the electric fan, and had seen the handkerchief tighten on the trigger, paying not the least attention to it, and not even realizing the significance of the pistol report for some moments, so accustomed was he to blank cartridges in his work. The Sheriff stared at him, after this glib and wholly convincing tale, in wonderment.

It must have been an hour before Dmitri was called, and he took his place in the chair with the air of one who had indeed played many tragic roles in his life, not all of them on the stage.

Prompted by the Coroner, he told once more the harrowing tale he had told in the afternoon. But he filled it with little variations, he noted how odd he had thought it that Vicki should insist on all this bother to understand a scene which was really the director's business anyway, a point he hadn't bothered to mention before. He told how he expostulated at the time it was taking, on the ground that he was hungry, a bit of evidence that drew a smile from all, even the Coroner. At one point the Sheriff interrupted sharply: "Are you trying to tell us that this here Adlerkreutz killed himself?"

"I don't know, Sharf. I really don't know. It was all very funny. I tell you, I feel sure I saw Tony take shell from a gun. How did one more shell enter this gun? Did Vicki put it there? I don't know. I only tell what happened."

The Coroner looked at him sharply, and said: "Wait a minute, wait a minute. You didn't say one word about this today."

"I was upset. I don't know what I said today."

"Did Adlerkreutz say anything about killing himself?"

"To me, no. Don't know about odder people."

Dmitri looked hopefully at Sylvia, but she was staring stonily at her gloved hands. He looked at the Sheriff, but got only a puzzled frown in return. The Coroner said: "I don't get this. A Coroner's jury is reluctant to return a verdict of suicide under any circumstances, but here you, without adding any item of evidence, make a lot of mysterious remarks about what you thought, and intimating that the deceased must have put the shell in the gun, and I don't understand it, that's all. Are you holding something back?"

"No, plizze, I hold nothing back."

"This is all conjecture."

"Con—"

"Just *guesswork?*"

"Absolutely, yes sir, guesswork."

Irritated, the Coroner led Dmitri through the rest of his story, encountered much less gabbiness. Dmitri stood down. Then he walked off to one side. Then, to his horror, he heard the Coroner say to his jury: "O.K., then as soon as the Sheriff identifies this other stuff for the record, I'll instruct you in the law and you can consider your verdict."

He caught Mr. Layton outside, between the parked cars, where he had followed when that gentleman got up and hurried out of the hearing. But when he grabbed Mr. Layton's arm, he was flung roughly against the side of the building. "So that's the kind of a cross you pull on me, hey? Get up there and mumble something about how funny it looks, and then go off in a corner, and that's supposed to make it a suicide, hey? Where's that letter she was supposed to get?"

"Plizze! We wrote the letter! We—"

"Then where is it?"

"I gave it to the Sharf! He took it! He—"

Waiting no longer, Mr. Layton strode off to the rear, no doubt to drag his surprise witness out of his car and parade her in to the Coroner. Dmitri didn't wait to see. He turned to the open window at his side, dropped his elbows on the sill, and quite unrestrainedly began to weep. He seemed to have his head in some kind of storeroom, and his tears splashed down on big green dice in an open box on the floor.

He was in a dreadful spot all right. But he had become part of a business that was accustomed to dreadful spots, and had been well schooled on what to do about them. When a crisis arises, some writer usually bellows: "I got it, I got it, I GOT IT! Cut to those sirens! Cut to those motorcycles coming down to street! Maybe it's not story, but it's ACTION!"

That may have been why Dmitri suddenly straightened up, fished a cigarette out of his pocket, lit it, and dropped it into the box of celluloid dice.

Chapter Eleven

The sirens were a success, quite as much of a success as they invariably are in a fast, gangster movie. They came screeching out from town at 80, motorcycles in front, the chief's car behind that, the salvage truck behind that, the ladder truck behind that, and the pump behind that, a fine, glittering, noisy, 100% American midnight motorcade. Even so, it was tame in comparison with what went on *inside* the Domino. The inflammable dice, if they had been all, might not have amounted to much, and Dmitri's desperate scheme might have failed for the simple reason that a fire takes a great deal longer to get going than a theatrical imagination realizes. But the box happened to be sitting within an inch or two of the big intake cable that led from the connection outside to the electric meter at rear. So when the dice flared hotly up they did not ignite the wall, for it was made of some sort of fireproof composition, but they did melt the cable, so that the first result of the cigarette was that the place went completely dark, without so much as a fuse blowing out. For a minute or so, as Americans versed in the idiosyncrasies of power houses, the gathering sat around without saying a word: one or two muttered gags about a blackout were rebuked by the coroner, who said it was not a frivolous occasion. But when another minute went by and no light came on, the Coroner said: "Well, we got to get on with this. Tony, do you think you could get us a few candles?"

"I'll do it."

It was the voice of one of the girl dealers, and at once there was the sound of her heels clicking off to a coroner, and then out. At once came her scream. and then another. "It's on fire, the whole storeroom is burning" she called, as soon as she could run back into the casino. At once came the Sheriff's voice: "Out, everybody. Take it easy. but get outside." The front door opened, making a big rectangular patch of light from outside, and Mr. Flynn's voice said: "This way." Several photographers. carrying cameras and evidently concerned for their pictures. hurried out. But hardly had Mr. Flynn spoken when Tony. frantically. yelled: "The cash! Girls, the cash! Girls, don't let me down without getting the cash out!" For the cash, amounting to several thousand dollars, had been rung up on the registers, but it had not been put in the safe, and Tony's voice betrayed only too well what he stood to lose if the place went up and took his precious paper with it.

Within a few seconds there was a frightful din, as the girls groped their way to the registers to retrieve the cash, the officers groped their way to the girls and tried to get them out, and the photographers groped their way inside again to take pictures of the scene by flashbulb, all yelling at the top of their lungs. But a dull, flickering glow took command at last, accompanied by the smell of smoke, and by the light of that, the girls ran out, handing their money to Tony at the door. After them stamped the irate officers. When the fire apparatus arrived, in answer to Mr. Britten's call, some of the crowd was out front, but most of it was at the side, watching Tony, Jake, and one or two others throwing water into the storeroom window with buckets.

Dmitri, being already out, took no part in any of these proceedings, but stood apart, some little distance off, apparently studying how best to take advantage of the diversion he had created. When the firemen piled off their trucks and began coupling their hoses to the plugs along the main highway, he spotted the Sheriff, standing with the first chief near the ladder truck. Going over and speaking in a large, confident way, he said: "Can I bother you one minute, Sharf?"

"About what?"

"Plizze, is confidential."

Wonderingly the Sheriff followed him a few steps off, until they were on the banks of the little mountain stream. Dmitri cleared his throat, said mysteriously and importantly: "Sharf, there was one thing. One thing I didn't tell when Excellenz ask me. Sharf, I feel sure this Vicki, this my friend, he killed himself."

"What you got to go on?"

"Last night he wrote a letter."

"How do you know?"

"He took my pen. My pen with green ink. He wrote a letter to Sylvià, put a special on, drove out and mailed it. Sharf, when he finish this letter Vicki cried. He cried like a baby. In my arms, he cried. Sharf, I *know* this man took his own life."

"Well, you could be right."

"What did she say when she read this letter, ha?"

"The letter you gave me?"

"Sure, it was the same one."

"She never saw it."

"She—What did you say?"

"I burned it up. She got kind of upset when I handed it to her. Broke her up. I didn't see any reason for making her feel worse. I pitched it on the fire. It's gone."

Dmitri made a noise like a very small pig. The Sheriff watched an emergency truck of the electric light company turn in at the gate, then turned a reflective eye on the wretched little figure in front of him. "You seem kind of upset yourself."

"Yes, Sharf. He was my friend."

"We'll never know."

He started to rejoin the fire chief, but Dmitri caught his arm. "No, Sharf, plizze don't go. I must talk to you."

"What about?"

"Money."

"In what way would you want to talk to me about money?"

"Man to man."

"You sure you don't mean crook to cop?"

"Why, that's ridiculous."

"Then say what it is."

"Now, Sharf, don't get sore, because I don't know how goes with you. Sometimes a guy needs money, sometimes now."

"He generally does."

"O. K., then if twanny five-fifty will help out, say the word, here I am. Cesh, or any way you want it."

"You think I could be bought for fifty bucks?"

"Bucks? Don't make me laugh. Grand."

Even the Sheriff, no stranger to matters cinematic, blinked at this gay riposte. "You mean you'd pay me fifty thousand dollars to cover up something in this case?"

"Cover up? Who said cover up?"

"Then for what?"

"That I can sleep my nights, Sharf. That I can go back to Hollywood and hold up my head. That I can look people in the eye. That they don't say, he let his friend be killed. That they don't say, there goes the dirty heel that didn't think any more of his friend than to let him use a loaded gun. That they don't say—"

"I got the idea."

"Sharf, I know this note says Vicki will take his own life if Sylwia gets a divorce. All I ask, Sharf, is that you tell you read note *first. Before* you burned it up, that's O. K. Who wouldn't? My God, to save a girl from feeling so bad, anybody would burn it up. You do this for me, so all know Dimmy Spiro is no heel, that all know Vicki himself did this, that's all I esk. No cover up. The truth, Sharf! The truth!"

The Sheriff cogitated over this some moments, staring at Dmitri, or at that spot a few inches behind Dmitri's head that seemed to be his focal point at certain moments. Then he said: "Here's where you get the surprise of your life. I'm taking your money."

"Sharf! Sharf! I die! From happy!"

"I want your check."

"Anything.

"Make it to Parker Lucas, Treasurer."

"Treasurer what?"

"Just at large."

"O. K., do like you say."

"I won't testify that you read the letter, but I'll testify there was a letter, and that I burned it. If you want to testify that you lent him the pen to write the letter, and that he cried and made remarks that led you think it was a suicide letter, then O. K., that's up to you. But I'll agree if the inquest turns out in a way that interferes with your sleep, to return your money."

"O. K., Sharf, it's wonderful!"

The Sheriff led the way to his car and got in, beckoning Dmitri to follow. Then he turned on the top light, and Dmitri got out a single blank check. Then, using the brim of the Sheriff's hat for a writing table, he wrote a check, handed it over. After examining it carefully, the Sheriff put it in his pocket.

"O. K., Mr. Spiro, thanks."

"Ah, Sharf, you don't know what you do for me."

"You set that fire?"

". . . What you say, Sharf?"

"I asked you if you set this place on fire."

"O. K., Sharf, I did."

"You're paying for that too. Every cent it takes to repair that damage, so Tony doesn't even put in a claim."

"Sharf, you know I will."

Chapter Twelve

The inquest, when it assembled in a quite battered showed every indication of frayed nerves. It was, and had been even before the fire, in the last few minutes of its life, and the jury, to say nothing of officers, witnesses, and newspaper men, wanted to get away. The Coroner rapped for order, and instructed the jury that they were to certify the fact of death, the cause of death, the manner of death, if they had been able to ascertain it, and any consequences of death they thought proper to include, particularly whether they knew of any persons who should be held for the grand jury. He was interrupted by the Sheriff, who asked permission to add to his testimony. He then said what he had promised Dmitri he would say. Dmitri was then permitted to testify about the letter, and especially the way his head would hang in shame if it were fastened upon him that he had been careless enough to let his friend be killed by accident, whereas in truth the affair had been a deliberate, if cunningly concealed suicide. The Coroner said: "You are to disregard the last two pieces of evidence, since conjecture, regard for personal feelings, or other irrelevant things don't concern you."

The jury whispered for two or three minutes, then one of the middle-aged men got up and said: "We find the said Victor Alexis Olaf Hermann Adlerkreutz came to his death by bullet through the heart fired from a gun in his own hands and the hands of Dmitri Spiro in an accidental and unintentional manner."

"So entered."

There was a stir as the newspaper people

stood up, and the Coroner opened his mouth to declare the inquest at an end.

"Just a minute."

The sound of moving feet toward the door stopped, and Dmitri caught the Sheriff's arm, whimpering, whispering, pleading. But the Sheriff paid no attention, being evidently interested in Mr. Layton, who was striding with masterful mien toward the Coroner's table. Then Dmitri did what was perhaps the first stupid thing he had done in a long and terrible day. As he hung to the Sheriff's arm, he saw a letter in the Sheriff's pocket. With Mr. Layton just a few feet away, and Ethel slithering her way forward in his wake, he evidently thought it no time to hesitate. Taking the letter between a roguish thumb and forefinger he flipped it out of the pocket and said: "Sharf, Sharf, you kid me! You didn't burn this note at all! You—"

But when he saw the envelope he stopped, and his face froze in horror. The Coroner, who had been whispering in puzzlement to Mr. Flynn, stopped too, he being no more than three feet away. For there, in the Sheriff's handwriting, were the words: "Shoreham Confession." Reaching out, he took the letter from Dmitri. Then, taking a knife from his pocket, and acting with grave, slow deliberation, he slit it open, took out the slip of paper that it contained, read it. Then, taking off his glasses and looking frighteningly solemn, he said: "Sheriff Lucas, Sylvia Shoreham, Tony Rico, Dmitri Spiro, and Gerland La Bouche, it is my duty to inform you that you are under arrest, that you must submit yourselves at once to search, and that anything you say here may be used against you."

No matrons were present to search Sylvia, but the Coroner swore in the Domino's phone girl, and instructed her what she was to take, what to leave on the prisoner. The two women then went off to the ladies' room. Police, expert on their job, made quick work of the men prisoners, while the reporters, still in the dark as to this unexpected twist, tried to break through the Coroner's silence for their deadlines. It wasn't until Sylvia and the phone girl returned, and a little memo book taken from her handbag had been placed on the table, that the Coroner resumed. Looking at the book, he handed it back to Sylvia; then, in a slow measured voice, read the confession.

It emptied it, as no fire could have done. The newspaper men stampeded for their deadlines in a noisy, shouting throng, and for a full minute after their departure the air outside was full of the noise of their taxis and cars. The Coroner, who had rapped angrily for order, waited until things quieted down. Then he turned to the prisoners and said: "Is there any statement any of you people wish to make?"

Heads went together and in a moment Mr. Daly said: "I came here, Doctor, to represent Miss Shoreham, but Mr. Rico, Mr. Spiro, and Mr. La Bouche have asked me to take charge for them too. On behalf of them, I inform you that I have advised them to stand on their constitutional rights."

Mr. Flynn said: "How shall I charge them?"

The Coroner said: "Murder, accessory after murder, suppression of evidence of murder, obstruction of justice, and perjury."

"Miss Shoreham didn't testify."

"Disjoin her from the perjury charge."

"What murder?"

The Coroner looked at the Sheriff in some annoyance. "Sheriff Lucas, are you in your right mind?"

140

"I am."

"The murder of Victor Adlerkreutz as confessed by Sylvia Shoreham in a statement that has just been taken from your pocket."

"That statement is not evidence."

"That's for the grand jury to determine."

"That statement was given me by Miss Shoreham on my threat to prosecute her sister for killing Victor Adlerkreutz."

"Why didn't you present it?"

"It's false."

"Or might this be the reason?" Mr. Flynn handed over, and the Coroner grimly accepted, a slip of paper.

"What is it?"

"It's a check. A check taken from your person when you were searched just now, signed by Dmitri Spiro, and made out to you."

"To me, as Treasurer."

"Of what? The Parker Lucas Benevolent Association?"

This got a laugh, but Sylvia suddenly looked up, as though it meant something to her. The Sheriff said: "Whatever I'm Treasurer of, the check's not evidence and don't concern this inquest."

"Bribery might interest the grand jury too."

"No bribery. Sorry, your honor. Bribery begins with the acceptance and retention of good and valuable things and it generally involves cash. A check proves an honest man. It's been gone into many times. A check is not evidence until it's cashed, and the cash is not evidence until it's kept. What I'm treasurer of I don't care to say at this time."

"If Miss Shoreham's sister committed this murder or you think she did, why didn't you put that facet in evidence?"

"There's been no murder."

"Sheriff Lucas, will you stop trifling with me?"

"I'm not trifling. Hazel Shoreham is dead."

The Sheriff related briefly the discovery of the girl's body earlier in the evening. Then he went on: "A homicide is not a murder until a jury says it is, and with the murderer dead no charge growing out of murder could ever be brought. Just the same, it seemed to me these picture people, in their desire to keep the Shoreham name out of this, had trifled with me and trifled with this state. The question was, how to get something on them, and I deliberately waited until the end of this inquest, or nearly the end of it, when I was going to break in on you with the truth, and then at least we'd have them for perjury. All, that is, except Miss Shoreham, since she didn't testify, but I didn't mind about her, because her effort to deceive me was at least from a motive no worse than trying to save her sister. But these men were concerned with money, the film they couldn't release if this scandal got out. So I was ready to shoot, but this man, this man Spiro here, crossed me up."

The Coroner's face had changed quite a lot during this laconic recital, and the jury obviously believed it. The Coroner, in a different tone, said: "How do you mean he crossed you, Parker?"

"By setting this fire."

"By—*what?*"

Tony jumped up with an exclamation, but Mr. Flynn rapped for order. The Coroner said: "Well! It's *one* thing we could get him for."

"*If* Tony prosecutes."

"You think I won't?"

"Yeah."

The Sheriff drawled this out with half-lowered eyelids, then added: "On account of you and Spiro being such good friends lately. You wouldn't cross a pal, would you?"

"I'd—have to think about it."

"I thought so."

The Sheriff turned to the Coroner, went on: "Friend Spiro set the fire to bust up the inquest until he could get me by the arm and try to buy me off. I couldn't to save my neck figure what he was up to, because I hadn't let out a peep yet, but when he said some more about suicide, and wanted me to say I'd read that note he talked bout here, I begun to smell insurance. And then I saw a way to get them all, and at the same time get our state what it's needed so bad all this time, that tuberculosis hospital. I told Spiro to make out his check to me as Treasurer. And I had reason to think that whatever was paid for accident, that wouldn't be paid for suicide, I could get *that* for our hospital too, and teach the insurance company a lesson. And I didn't have to be told how much I could tap Tony for and this La Bouche, and maybe some others of them that had been trying to make suckers out of us."

"Parker, you went too far."

"Who says I did? We got one of the funniest states in this Union. It's a big state, and once it was a rich state. Now it's not, and only a few people live in it, but we all know those mines are going to come back, and I speak for every man, woman, and child in it when I say we all made up our minds long ago that we weren't going to let it go to pot while we were waiting for whatever is in store. We've kept our state clean and given our children schools and our motorists roads but we had to do it our own way. We couldn't do it with taxes because we didn't collect enough. We did it with divorce and gambling and other things you all know about but I won't go into here. We give them the decentest divorce, the squarest gambling, and the best-regulated things of other kinds, that you find anywhere. We went on the principle our state's preservation was involved, and if it was in the public interest and nobody got hurt, it was all right. You mean to tell me it's not the same way here?"

Nobody answered. The Sheriff went on: "Now it's been broke wide open, and a verdict of accident is out. Just the same, if this idiot hadn't pulled this so-called confession out of my pocket, it would have given us our hospital, and everybody would have been taught all the lesson that was necessary."

"You think so?"

Mr. Layton, who had been completely forgotten these last few minutes, now stepped truculently forward. To the Sheriff he said: "So, with a signed confession from her on you, it's the other sister. With a fifty-grand bribe on you, it's just taking up a collection for t.b. patients. With Hazel Shoreham made the murderer of Victor Adlerkreutz, instead of the beneficiary, Sylvia Shoreham, the Southwest General of N. A. is hooked fifty thousand dollars of life insurance, hey? Not while I'm here we're not. Your honor, I'd like to present a witness. One that'll tell who *really* killed Victor Adlerkreutz."

As Ethel, motioned on by Mr. Layton, came diffidently forward, there were many exchanges of glances, and the Coroner said to the Sheriff: "There's nothing I can do but hear her."

"I should say not."

The Coroner told Ethel to be seated, asked her to hold up her right hand, swore her in. He had Mr. Flynn take her name, uneasily asked Mr. Pease if he wanted to take over the examination. Mr. Pease said he was doing very well himself, and should continue. He told Ethel that since he had no idea what she knew, perhaps the best thing would be for her to tell her story in her own way, and she did so, with a breathless, beady-eyed earnestness that could no more

146

be doubted than a train-announcer could be doubted.

She said she dealt a game of blackjack that morning to a foreign gentleman known to her as Vic, though she had no idea he was Sylvia Shoreham's husband. Then, she said, Jake the bartender whispered to her, Sylvia Shoreham was in the office. She was that excited, she said, that she couldn't count her chips, and paid Vic $1 to which he was not entitled. Soon, she said, Jake came out and called Vic and Vic went into the office, but she had no chance to go look because as soon as she rang up her cash three gentlemen came in and one of them wanted to play with $1 chips. She pointed to Mr. La Bouche as the high-limit customer, and then went on: "He played and he played and he played, and he lost $50 and wanted to get it back and all the time I seen Tony trotting in with a champagne set-up and I knew something was going on and I almost went wild. Then the little man looked at his watch and said come on, and this gentleman cashed his chips and all three went in the office. Then I started to go in. I was going to make out like there was two chips missing and this gentleman should look and if he had them in his pocket I'd give him cash, and then while he was looking I was going to hand my lipstick to Miss Shoreham and ask her to autograph my apron. But then Tony, he seen what I was up to, and said beat it back to my table."

"When was this?"

"Around ten-thirty."

"Go on."

"So then they drove off."

"Who drove off?"

"First Vic, and then Miss Shoreham. And then Mr. Spiro, he played roulette while he was having his boots shined. Vic went in his car and Miss Shoreham went in Tony's car. But then, it took about an hour, here she came back. She parked in front but didn't come in the casino. That meant she had gone in the office the side way. So then Vic's car came back with the lights on and some girl was driving and she let Vic out and then turned the car around and waited. So Vic come in the casino and went over and said something to Mr. Spiro and Tony told him his ring was in his office and he went in there. I kept watching Tony till he went out back and I started for the office door."

"When was this?"

"Some time after twelve."

"Did you go in?"

"No, sir. I put my hand on the knob, but then I could hear her voice and something told me to stay out. I couldn't hear what she was saying but it had a funny note in it. So the slot wasn't quite shut, the door that closes it I mean, and I peeped. I could only see that corner where the desk is, but she was over there, carrying on and carrying on and carrying on. Then she stopped and began looking for matches to light a cigarette. She opened the middle drawer and tried to bang it shut and caught her dress. So then she did bang it shut. So then she opened the righthand drawer, where the guns are kept. I seen this look come over her face and then she took out a gun and raised it. Then Vic was between me and her and then he was up there beside her talking to her and she put the gun down—"

"Wait a minute, wait a minute."

The Sheriff turned to Mr. Flynn: "Did Miss Shoreham, Miss Sylvia Shoreham, come into my office this morning?"

"She did, yes sir."

"How was she dressed?"

"Gray slacks, blue sweater, red ribbon around her hair, red shoes. We was talking about them slacks after she left, me and Dobbs and Hirsch."

To Ethel, the Sheriff said: "Describe the dress."

"It was green, with small brass buttons."

"It wasn't slacks?"

"She didn't have on slacks at all."

To a young officer, the Sheriff said: "Enders."

"Yes, sir."

"You had charge of the Hazel Shoreham case?"

"That's right, sir."

"You saw the body removed from the car?"

"I lifted it out myself."

"How was that girl dressed?"

"Light cream colored spring coat, brown shoes, light stockings, no hat, green dress with small brass buttons. The dress is in Mr. Daly's car. In the valise we put in there for Miss Shoreham."

There was a stir as two officers went outside, came back with the valise, and opened it. The effects that had been taken from the dead girl correspond with the Enders description. Mr. Flynn opened an envelope, said to the Coroner: "Little snag of green silk we found jammed in that drawer." The Coroner lifted the dress, found a little hole over the right hip from which the snag had been torn. He turned angrily to Ethel. "What's the idea, coming up here at this hour at night, lying like that?"

"She's not lying."

Sylvia, over the protests of Mr. Daly, blotted tears from her eyes and said: "It all happened exactly as she says, and I'm sure she thought it was I she was looking at. My sister looked a great deal like me. She was often mistaken for me."

"What was she carrying on about?"

It was some seconds before Sylvia answered, and then a hush fell over the crowd that wasn't broken at once. She said: "She was insane."

". . . She killed your husband?"

"Yes. I didn't actually see it. I had my back turned. But there can't be any doubt about it. Then I decided I was going to say I did it, and I made her leave, so nobody would find her there."

The tears were streaming down Sylvia's face now, so it was some time before anybody remembered Ethel. Then the Coroner said; "Well—let's let this girl finish. All right, she put the gun down."

"She put it down, and Vic put it back. But then she picked it up again and put it in her mouth. I opened my mouth to scream, because I knew she was going to kill herself, but Vic grabbed the gun and got it out of her mouth and then it went off and—"

"What?"

The two voices, saying the same word, cut Ethel off, Sylvia's voice vibrant with joy, Mr. Layton's with utter consternation. Then Sylvia broke into a little sobbing laugh. "Thank God, thank God,—I might have known she never deliberately killed anybody. She was too sweet. Then she ran over, put her arms around Ethel, and kissed her.

From the shadows, with a sic-Semper-Tyrranis clang-tint, came Dmitri's voice: "Sylwia Shoreham is windicated! SYLWIA SHOREHAM IS WINDICATED!"

In a hotel bedroom, in the black hour before dawn, a phone was ringing. A woman dressed in mourning entered, answered, said: "Send him up." Then she went into a dark sitting room, opened the door into the hall, and sat down before a fire that had burned down to red embers. Soon there was a tap and she said: "Come." A tall man came in, closed the door, and stood uncertainly before her, near the fire. He said: "I didn't want to wait till tomorrow before asking you about those bodies."

"My husband was Dimmy's friend. I think he'd prefer that Dimmy took over the funeral. My sister—do I have to say at once?"

"Whatever you decide, if you'll call my office there'll be somebody there that'll attend to everything without you being put to any trouble."

"That is very thoughtful of you."

"And I want to apologize."

"We started the day with an apology."

"For shooting past a big moment in your life, without knowing it was a big moment. That's what you said. And that's what I have to apologize for now, except that my big moment was a much bigger moment than yours was, and it was also a big chance, an opportunity, and I didn't have sense enough to know it. If I had just had a little faith in you, I might have known that there was some explanation, that your sister was being mistaken for you in these hotels."

"Even if I deliberately deceived you?"

"Yes. And—I come to say goodbye." He stood awkwardly a few moments, perhaps wondering if she would offer her hand. When she didn't and when she made no reply, he turned, took one or two slow, heavy steps toward the door.

"Parker?"

He turned, and she said, "Come here." When he was near to her she took both his hands in hers, pulled him down beside her on the little two-seater that faced the fire. "What are you talking about, goodbye? After the way you stood by me there at the hearing, and cleared me, and all the rest of it! And let me tell you something; If I ever found out that you had got those reports, and didn't all but kill me, I'd never forgive you. Now: Did you blackjack any money for your hospital? Is that what you were doing out there all this time."

They all contributed a generous amount."

"How much insurance do I get?"

"That was the funny part. After tearing in like a wolf, they were just as friendly as you could imagine when the jury came in with practically the same verdict, 'in an accidental and unintentional manner' with nothing but the names changed. The chief claim adjuster, man by the name of Gans, said: 'We'll go the limit to hang it on you if you used loaded dice—we mean you play straight, because we do. But *if* you play straight, we'll pay any just claim quick as any other gambler pays off, and with no more griping. We don't have to gripe, or gyp. The percentage is working for us, and we've got to win.' You'll collect a hundred thousand in all."

"Then I'll give that, and fifty I have saved up, to the hospital. Altogether, now, how much does that make?"

"Little over quarter million."

"That's a start."

"It assures the institution."

". . . About Hazel."

"Just say, and I'll attend to it."

"I don't know whether to keep her here, or send her back to California. You see, I'll want her with me, and—"

"You staying here?"

"I might be getting married."

He took her in his arms, held her close, looked at her gravely, almost reverently. Then he said: "I'm going in the army."

"So am I."

"Doing what?"

"Nursing I think."

Presently he said: "Up to this minute, I been a little bit in love with Edith Cavell, as well as Sylvia Shoreham. Now I'm not. I'm all in love with you. Because listen: I want you to go in the army. I want you to be a nurse. But I don't want you to wind up like Edith Cavell did. You hear what I'm telling you?"

"I'll wind up as I wind up."

". . . That's right."

"When do you go in the army?"

"Twentieth of next month."

"Then the day after that, I go. But—until then, can't we be with each other? Can't I be here with you?"

"The sun's coming up."

"So it is."

"Come on, I want you to see your home."

In the gray dawn, a car slowed down on a deserted road, and turned in at the stone posts that marked the entrance of a ranch. In it were a man and a woman, saying nothing, sitting very close.